his reputation

A LOVE GAMES NOVEL
by
ALLYSON LINDT

For my eternal dragon

chapter one

There were times when Kenzie envied her sister's ability to slide into new relationships. Admired the way Riley always found the guys who knew how to have fun. Wished she could let loose like her twin.

Her envy tended to evaporate when Riley showed up on her doorstep at midnight—the way she had last night—cheeks smeared with tears and mascara, bags in hand and looking for a place to crash.

Kenzie inched forward with the line in the coffee shop, focused more on her thoughts than the Saturday morning crowds pushing in on her. Once she had her tea, she could concentrate on all the ways her love life wasn't pathetic. First way was… *Nope, total blank.*

Okay, that was a failed exercise.

An hour ago Kenzie had tried to dig for more information. To help. To nudge Riley into spilling what had gone wrong and maybe offer a little advice in return. Her reward? Insults.

Riley's words echoed in Kenzie's thoughts, taunting her in rhythm with the chatter of people around her. Kenzie wasn't frigid. She'd been the one to leave her last boyfriend for not delivering on the excitement in the bedroom. Just because she was picky about the men she dated didn't mean she was uptight. Refusing to go out with anyone who thought chartreuse was a flavor of frozen yogurt didn't make her a bad person.

And preferring her men clean and publicly presentable didn't mean she lacked imagination.

When Kenzie reached the front counter, glass cases filled with pastries mocked her. The plum tarts looked good, but indulging a sugar craving wasn't the way to sate her wounded ego. She ordered a large peppermint tea. The room dimmed as clouds outside drifted in front of the sun.

She grabbed her drink and scanned the crowded room for a place to sit and sip. Not a single unoccupied table, but three had available seats. A woman sat at the first, trying to force-feed the baby in her lap a pacifier while Mom sucked on a latte. At the second, two teenage boys stared at their phones, their only verbal conversation the occasional laughter as they smacked each other on the arm.

Then there was the scenery at table three.

The man with a shock of brown, spiked hair, broad shoulders, and a tattered T-shirt that looked like it had seen one too many accidental bleachings dominated a table in the corner of the room, one of the few empty chairs next to him. The clothes made him look twenty, but he held himself with a confidence that made her think he was actually older than her twenty-six.

She had no idea who he was, but she saw him

almost every weekend, and used the fact he was frequently engrossed in something on his phone or some game device as an excuse to study him without getting caught staring.

What's keeping you from approaching him? The question taunted her in Riley's voice. It wasn't as if she was shy.

The answer was painfully obvious. *It's not appropriate.* Women didn't hit on random men in coffee shops.

Riley would. Hell, Riley would have had his number weeks ago, and probably been living with him just a few days later.

Kenzie took a deep breath. She could at least strike up a conversation and see where things went from there. She approached the empty spot before she could talk herself out of it, and forced confidence into her voice. "Excuse me."

"Hmm?" He barely moved his head, immersed in something on his phone.

"Is this seat taken?"

He pulled his attention from the screen long enough to rake his gaze over her. Her breath caught at the deep brown of his eyes. *Gorgeous.* Just as quickly, he turned back to his phone. A flicker of a smile tugged up the corner of his mouth. "It's not taken yet, but I'm hoping you'll have a seat and solve that problem."

What now? She'd never played the role of aggressor before, but she was already realizing it was easier to be the one doing the turning down than the one doing the asking.

"Do you come here often?" She winced at the

pathetic line the moment it was out.

He spared her another glance, laughter dancing on his face. "Probably at least as often as you."

And that was it. He was buried in his distraction again.

How embarrassing. She exhaled. This wasn't worth the effort, but it would look awkward if she left so soon. She should at least use the seat she'd secured. Grabbing her phone, she pulled up the book she'd been in the middle of and tried to lose herself in the pages while she drank her tea.

Background noise screamed around her, and she pushed it aside. A creeping heat flooded her face as something tickled her senses. Was someone watching her? She looked up, startled to see the man across from her glancing between the phone and her.

She shifted her attention from her book—Scott assumed it was a book since she was staring at a white screen with lots of black letters. Her piercing blue eyes were curious, and a hard line disrupted the swelling in her flushed lips. It was time to forget the game he was testing for work.

He'd noticed her before. The long legs, narrow waist, and round ass accentuated her jeans the way the over-priced designer had intended, and the entire package was always nice to look at. But the fact that her wardrobe screamed *I don't mind overpaying for a label* reminded him of too many women he dated who preferred his wallet to his company.

"Is something wrong?" She stared back, face quirked in question.

He'd been surprised and curious when she approached, and amused by the hesitation coming from a woman who held herself with so much confidence. It was a shame she let the conversation die when he went to save his game, and he was hoping to reinitiate it. Find out more about this potential dichotomy.

"Nothing's wrong." He met her steady gaze, keeping his tone even but not able to hide all his amusement. "Just wondering something."

She ducked her head, gaze falling to his hand before it quickly jumped back to his face. "What's that?"

The flush on her cheeks was enticing. How much redder could he make her go before she slapped him? Or let him brush his mouth over hers. He nodded at her phone. "How contrived their happily ever after is."

"Excuse me?"

Yup, she was going to slap him. Or at least grind her heel into his toes. Thank the open-source gods she wore sneakers and not heels.

"The big tough hero and his dainty mistress." He knew better than to assume, but that had never stopped him in the past, and everything about her, from the way she'd folded a napkin on her knee to the ponytail that didn't look like it would budge even with a solid, impassioned tug, screamed repressed. "Is he a duke? Or maybe she's a stripper with a heart of gold?" One of his two best friends, Rae, was forever losing herself in romance novels. He adored her, but never understood her fascination with the books. Reality wasn't happily ever after.

His tablemate rolled her eyes and slid the phone across the table. "*He's* a teenager who was psychologically tortured by Homeland Security for more than a week, and *she's* helping him get back at *the man*."

That sounded familiar. He tapped the screen to bring up the book information. *Little Brother*. His smile turned genuine. "My mistake. Good book, I won't spoil the ending."

The ambivalence in her half-formed smile stole his next breath. Her tone was dry. "I appreciate it. Sorry to disappoint you, but bad euphemisms aren't my thing."

This was fun. "Really? Sacred vees and turgid manhood—or is it manhoods, plural? Or maybe that's a different kind of story. That doesn't do anything for you?"

She dropped the phone into her purse, mouth still twitching in indecision. Damn that was a good look for her.

"Not on paper." She ran a tongue over her bottom lip before catching it between her teeth.

He wouldn't mind giving that a try. Nipping at that full almost-pout. His pulse sped up at the banter. He pushed his game aside and leaned in, fingers clasped and hands resting on the table. He was going to enjoy this for as long as she wanted to keep it up. The last couple of women he'd been with—hell, even his last couple of girlfriends before that—had been more giggle than brain. Cared more about how they looked on his arm than what he had to say.

He was sick of fake girls only interested in his money. This woman though, she radiated intelligence, genuineness, and had no idea who he was. "They were wrong. It's not more fun than a gorgeous woman."

"They?" Her flush spread to her neck.

Long, slender. What would it be like to run his tongue along that slope? "Marketing. They're making promises they can't keep." He pushed his half-eaten donut aside. Her bold responses mingled with the hesitation and embarrassment, flushing her pale skin, and all of it short circuiting his thoughts. He wanted more. "So you'd rather the exploration of honeyed walls took place in real life."

Disbelief mingled with her laughter. "Are you always so forward?"

Frequently, to the dismay of his board of directors. Another shadow passed through the shop as clouds covered the sun outside for a moment. "Only until it gets me slapped. You?"

"Always and for as long as I can get away with it." She shifted in her seat, leaning in, arms resting on the table and accentuating full breasts.

He forced his attention to stay on her face. She wasn't even close to the prissy socialite he'd imagined. It had been a long time since he pegged someone so completely wrong, and he was enjoying the hell out of it.

Her phone interrupted, a tinny pop song cutting through the veil of innuendo. She gave him an apologetic glance. "I'm sorry."

He waved a dismissive hand. "No worries. If it's your boyfriend asking you to talk dirty to him, go ahead."

"Not likely. No boyfriend." She answered the

phone. "What? …I stopped for tea someplace where they weren't going to snap at me for being nice." She glanced at him, hesitation in her eyes, and then shook her head. "Fine, okay. I'll be back in a little bit."

She dropped her phone in her purse and turned to him. "I'd love to stay longer, talk about whether or not one's manhood can actually throb, but I have to go."

"Shame. I might have proposed a hands-on experiment." He shoved the rest of his donut in his mouth and washed it down with a swallow of coffee.

"Does talking like that ever get you in trouble?"

"Let's just say I'm willing to take my chances in some cases." He stood and offered her a hand. "I should probably get back to real life too. I'll walk you out."

His hand lingered on her arm as he guided her through the crowds toward the exit, her warm skin against his sending pulsing tingles through him. When they stepped onto the sidewalk, the din of Saturday morning traffic rushed in to replace the chatter of inside. "Where did you park?" He was pretty sure he'd never seen her drive—it was hard to miss those things on mornings when the place was deserted except for the two of them—but it was polite to ask.

"Home."

That was a more vague answer than he was looking for, but it wasn't as if he wanted to meet her family. Or her cats. Whatever. His hand moved to the small of her back, nudging her across the parking lot. She didn't resist.

"Do you want a lift?" he asked.

Her footsteps slowed, and she pulled away. "In the love van?"

He spun to face her, not sure what to make of the comment. She'd nicknamed his car? *Fascinating.* "Excuse me?"

She nodded at the Escalade in the back of the parking lot. "That one's yours right? The Game God license plate? The tinted windows meant to keep out even the most penetrating light?"

She knew what the G4M3G0D on his plates meant. She was full of entertaining surprises. He bit back the urge to joke about the word *penetrating.* "That's it, but love van, really?"

She fell into step beside him again. "I can't be the only person who's called it that."

"To my face at least. Interesting assumption." He moved closer, letting his bare arm brush hers.

"No worse than deciding I was reading some bodice ripper inside."

He stopped at his SUV, spinning to face her and leaning back against it, one foot propped up on the rubber strip running along the bottom of the door. He looped his thumbs in his pockets. "Fair enough. We're even on the inappropriate assumption front then?"

She kept her distance but didn't seem in a hurry to leave. "I didn't know we were keeping score."

A gust of wind tore through the parking lot and whipped her ponytail into her face. She hugged herself and shivered as the clouds devoured the last traces of direct sunlight.

He forced his hands to stay by his side, biting his tongue before he could offer to warm her up. Or ask if she'd like to be the one biting his tongue. "Someone's always keeping score."

"Clever." A sharp chill wove itself into the wind, and she rubbed the visible goose bumps on her arms. Even through her bra, he could see her nipples were hard nubs, adding new geography to her fitted T-shirt.

He shouldn't be staring. Or imagining pulling her close, running his hands over those peaks, warming her up. He clicked the locks off on his car, yanked the door open, and grabbed his jacket off the back seat.

"Hmm…" Her voice was closer than she expected. "Clean. Beige leather. No shag carpet." He turned and she stepped back, ducking her head. "I had to see for myself."

"Sorry to disappoint you." He draped the fleece over her shoulders, and pulled the neck closed, hands lingering on her collarbone. The soft fruit of her shampoo mingled with a flowered perfume. He pushed back the urge to pull her closer, breathe her in, and taste her.

"Not disappointed at all."

Even though she was only a few inches shorter than his six two, she almost swam in the coat, the bottom hanging halfway down her thighs. An image flashed through his mind of her wearing nothing but that jacket, standing in his bedroom doorway—

A sharp bolt lit up the sky, accompanied by the concussive boom of thunder. She jumped, eliminating a few more inches between them, and laughed nervously, hand flying to her chest. "Holy crap."

His heart was hammering too, but not from the sudden noise. She stood near enough her warmth drifted toward his bare arms. Her gaze met his, and his breath caught. Such a captivating face.

A drop of rain landed on her cheek, then trailed down the smooth skin. He rested a hand on the back of her neck, thumb brushing away the water. His pulse raced even faster when she tilted her head into the gesture.

Another drop landed on her nose, her forehead, her chin. What would she do if he kissed them away?

The sky opened up, buckets pouring down, plastering his shirt to him in seconds.

She pulled his jacket tighter. "I think I'll take that ride after all."

He didn't argue, yanking open the passenger door and making sure she was inside before sprinting to the driver's side.

chapter two

Kenzie twisted in the leather seat to face him, sinking into the oversized jacket draping her shoulders and wiping the rain from her face. The faint scent of his cologne swam through her thoughts. She studied him, soaking wet, shirt accentuating every line of definition on his chest.

He laughed and raked his fingers through his brown spikes, pushing the dripping strands off his forehead. "So you'd rather take your chances in the love van than the rain? At least now I know your limits. You're not worried I might be bad news?"

"I know you're bad news." The way he didn't filter his thoughts, but was still gentle and polite. The hint of mischief always lurking in his smile and promising something unknown. It was making her giddy, and nervous, and tingly all over.

She worked her fingers into the elastic holding her hair back and yanked it free, letting the loose strands fall around her shoulders. The ponytail had kept it from getting soaked, and it was nice to have the almost-dry warmth against her skin. She'd rather it was his hand again, but the moment seemed to be gone.

How had she ended up in this man's car in the pouring rain, toeing the line of indecent conversation and fantasizing about stripping off his wet clothes? "The barista knows me. She saw us leave together."

"So they'll come after you when they find my body dead and mangled in a gutter?" His teasing smirk never faded.

She batted her eyelashes. "Yes. And the police will track me down, bringing my long string of kidnapping devastatingly sexy men to an end."

"Sexy?" He leaned closer, tucking a strand of hair behind her ear.

Crap, she hadn't meant to say that. No, wait, this was perfect. She wasn't being frigid anymore. She could do flirting. Especially when he made it so easy. Her voice was husky when she replied. "Definitely sexy."

"And you're going to devastate me?" His fingers lingered on her ear, tracing light lines, eyes searching hers. She inhaled sharply when he trailed down to her earlobe and then brushed the hollow behind it where her neck met her jaw.

Her heart hammered against her ribcage, and her mind argued with itself—half insisting this was grossly inappropriate and the other half saying she was thinking too much. He was a random stranger, not a client or an associate. Just a guy whose rough palm against her neck was driving her thoughts wild. "I wouldn't mind trying."

Wind howled against the vehicle, rain slamming into it from all sides and drowning out the rest of the world. She could get lost in those eyes.

"Don't you need to get home?" He didn't pull

away, and his skin was hot against hers.

The same argument she'd had with herself when Riley called echoed in her thoughts, but this time she was leaning toward continuing to swap one-liners with the sexy stranger instead of trudging back to her condo.

She shifted her weight in the seat and leaned into his hand, her voice almost lost in the storm outside. "Right. I should do that."

The corner of his mouth twitched, fingertips gliding along the back of her neck. "You're not convincing me."

She exhaled at the light touch, currents of anticipation flowing through her. "I haven't convinced myself."

"Maybe I can help tip the scales in my favor." He dipped his head and brushed his lips over hers.

She whimpered and scooted closer, returning the kiss. His mouth was hot against hers, his muffled chuckle ending in a groan when she nipped at his bottom lip. His fingers tangled in her hair, tongue probing her mouth. Her hand rested on his chest, and she traced the bulk that was solid muscle.

He tugged her head back with a hungry growl, tongue gliding down her jaw and neck, resting in the hollow at the base of her throat. His words vibrated against her skin. "If I'd thought things out..." He kissed along her collarbone, teeth grazing the soft skin where her shoulder met her neck. "I might have actually made this a love van."

She arched her back when his fingers danced up her spine. She pressed her chest into his, the rough texture of damp fabric biting into her skin. The sensation was enticing, but left her wanting the clothes out of the way completely. "I can't believe it's never come up before."

His laugh was a low rumble, laden with lust. He pushed the bottom of her shirt up, caressing her waist. "Trust me, that's not an issue now. It's up."

The innuendo was horrible but alluring. A bold voice in her thoughts drove her and overrode her hesitation. Her fingers dropped to his leg, caressing the inside of his thigh, damp denim harsh against the pads of her fingertips. "You mentioned something earlier about a hands-on experiment?"

He growled against her shoulder, and his hand moved to the front of her shirt, sliding up her stomach. "Now you're just teasing me."

She squirmed under his touch, need growing hot between her legs. "Now? What were we doing before?"

His thumb dipped under her bra, brushing the bottom of her breast. She gasped and moved her hand higher up his thigh. Part of her was intensely aware of how public their parking spot was. The other half wanted to slide his seat back and straddle his legs. Both halves agreed she didn't want to stop.

He kissed her again, and she pressed back, hungry. She massaged the inside of his leg, moaning with need.

A familiar ringtone echoed through the car, and she cursed her sister for picking now to call back.

"Do you need to get that?" His strong grip held her in place.

"She'll wait." Kenzie glided her hand higher, brushing his erection through his jeans.

He hissed and pulled her closer, almost throwing her off balance and forcing her to lean into him to keep from falling off the seat.

A digital chirp filled the car, mingling with the fading tones of Kenzie's phone.

"And that would be my keeper calling." His hands slid down her arms, and he pushed her upright, his face flushed and breathing heavy. "In case you didn't know, weekend work emergencies suck."

He knew that without taking the call? Her brows knit together, and she couldn't hide her disappointment. "You can't maybe ignore them for a couple minutes?"

"I can't think of anything that would make my weekend brighter." He tangled his fingers in her hair, kissing her hard one more time before sinking back into his seat and exhaling loudly. "I can put it off long enough to drop you off, but not long enough to give you a ride."

She understood making sacrifices for a job, but the last snippet of innuendo didn't dilute the disappointment washing over her. She sat back in her own seat. "Completely understand."

He grasped her fingers between his, kissing her knuckles. "But if it helps any, you're now officially my favorite fantasy."

The gesture sent flutters through her chest, and the words brought the fading heat rushing back to her face and every other inch of her body. "Ditto."

Riley was sitting on the couch, arms folded, pale face drawn into a scowl, when Kenzie pushed into the apartment.

"Where have you been?" Riley demanded. "You weren't answering your phone. I thought maybe something bad happened." She sat straighter, aggravation fading to curiosity. "Who does the jacket belong to?"

Kenzie couldn't keep the grin from her face. Even her sister's glower wasn't enough to spoil the residual tingles. "I don't know. I didn't get his name."

Riley's shoulders relaxed, and she leaned back into beige cushions. "Really? Spill."

Kenzie's smile grew, and she raked her fingers through her hair, working out some of the tangles. She shouldn't say it, but she couldn't help herself. "There's not much to tell. Guy from the coffee shop gave me a lift home. Things may or may not have gotten intense enough to steam up his windows before he dropped me off."

Riley's jaw dropped. "Mackenzie Carter, are you yanking my chain?"

Kenzie flushed. Finally, she had shocked her sister. And she was considering doing it again. She did need to give Mr. G4M3G0D back his jacket, and she knew where he spent a lot of his Saturday mornings. "Completely serious."

Riley smirked. "I don't need details. Unless he was hot. Like super, extra sexy."

Kenzie's mouth twisted, and she stared back at her sister. "He wasn't bad. He had a nice car. That's sexy, right?"

Riley didn't look impressed. "So in other words he was kind of bland and dim-witted. Not so much out of the ordinary for you after all."

Kenzie glared at her twin, not liking the implication. "He was gorgeous, intelligent, and did incredible things with his fingers." And lips, and mouth, and tongue. "Better?"

Riley rolled her eyes, dragged herself from the couch, and brushed past her, talking as she padded into the guest bedroom. "Whatever. Keep trying to build up the lie, and you might start to believe it. I know I don't."

Kenzie spun, glaring at her sister's back and struggling to remember why she'd hurried home. Her phone rang, postponing the irritation. She knew from the ringtone it was work. It wasn't like them to call on a Saturday.

"This is Mackenzie." She adopted her most professional tone.

"What's your calendar look like for the next few months?" her boss, Greta, asked.

The lack of formality didn't surprise Kenzie. Greta didn't believe in small talk.

She didn't hesitate to accept the offer. As a contractor, work meant getting paid, and she was trying to pad her bank account as much as possible. Early retirement wouldn't pay for itself, and if she stuck to her plan, in a decade she'd be spending her time in a remote villa south of the equator. "I've got some room, what's up?"

"We've got someone requesting a presentation Monday. They think it's an emergency. For you, it's standard stuff—out-of-control executive making his company look bad needs to learn how to act like an adult in public, that kind of stuff."

Monday didn't give her much time to prepare, but she was used to bouncing with emergency clients. She had a sales pitch on standby that she could slide into without a problem. "I'm on board. Send me the info and I'll be there."

"Already done." The line went dead.

Kenzie shrugged and flipped over to her email, scanning the guy's basic profile. Scott McAllister. Chief technical officer and half owner of a successful international software company, public bad boy. Great, a geek who didn't know how to hold himself around his peers. As long as he was pliable, the job would be easy.

She clicked the email shut. She could read the rest later. This was a no-brainer job. She should really try and make amends with her sister and find out what happened the night before.

Images and sensations still lingered on her skin from the stolen time in the stranger's SUV. And maybe spend some more time dwelling on what had happened that morning.

Scott pulled to a stop at the red light. He flopped his head back onto the headrest, not able to shake his smile. Completely anonymous, completely hot, and surprisingly brilliant. He was going to be using that memory for a while, wishing business hadn't interrupted the most fun he'd had with a woman in ages.

His phone rang. Speaking of business and interruptions. That would be Zach's fifth attempt to reach him in the last fifteen minutes. Time to face the music. He hit a button on his stereo, switching off the music and switching on the Bluetooth, hands-free system. "Hey."

"Care to tell me about Vegas?" Zach's hollow growl filled the interior of the SUV.

That had taken at least a day longer than it should have. Scott had been back in town since last night, and it had been at least thirty-six hours since the incident. Still there was no reason to fess up unless they were both thinking of the same thing. "You know what they sa—"

"Wrong." Zach cut him off. "I swear, if you say *what happens in Vegas stays in Vegas*, you're in charge of employee reviews for the next six months."

Scott's mouth twisted in disappointment. It was an effective threat. "Lame. But fine. What did you hear?"

"Uh uh." A loud exhale filtered through the speakers. Zach was smoking. This was bad. Zach never smoked on phone calls. "You tell me what happened so I know if there's shit that hasn't hit the fan yet."

Scott sighed and tucked away the mental images of coffee-shop woman for use later. "It wasn't a big deal. I stopped by the Digital Media booth to see what they've got going on. One of the girls was friendly, so we chatted. She may or may not have slipped me her room key. How was I supposed to know their VP of marketing was tapping that? Besides, it wasn't like I was going to." She'd laughed at all his jokes, but he'd had serious doubts she'd understood them.

Zach growled. "Tell me how this led to you pissing off one of our board members to the point he's threatening your job."

Scott's didn't have to ask who. Hank Cartee wanted his job every other week. It wasn't much of a threat. "I swear anyone watching thought the entire thing was staged. He insulted me, I insulted better. And maybe louder. Just like that dumb-ass game of theirs with the stupid-as-hell gangsters who all sound like Harvard graduates. What was I supposed to do, let him call me a hack and just walk away?"

"Yes." The single syllable was distinct. "You know how many eyes were there. How many people were watching."

Maybe that was why Hank had canceled their meeting after. Scott kept the thought to himself. "So?"

"This is getting old, Scott." Zach exhaled again, the breath echoing off the microphone. "The industry already thinks we're a couple of incompetent kids who got lucky, and this isn't helping. Hank is serious this time."

Scott snarled silently at the speakers, glad Zach couldn't see him. Hank was serious every time. A forty-something trust-fund baby from California with a bigger stick up his ass than…

Finishing the thought would just piss him off more, and he wanted to retain at least some of the buzz from coffee-shop girl. Still. The board was comprised of their investors—the reason they had enough cash to do what they did—so he should at least try and sound contrite. "I'm sorry."

"How sorry?" Something shifted in Zach's

tone.

Scott hesitated; he was about to be manipulated. He might as well get it over with. "Very, very sorry. I know what Cartee has done for us."

"All right, I'll accept that. You coming over tonight?"

Scott glanced at the speaker spewing the disembodied voice, concern flooding through him. There was no way the conversation was over that easily. "As long as you're not cooking."

"Well, Rae's not. She's prepping for a meeting with the board, showing them pretty numbers that remind them we're not morons."

Double shit. Scott pulled into the parking garage beneath his building. "Are you done stretching this out yet?"

"Not yet." Zach's smirk was almost visible over the phone. "You can sweat a little longer."

"I'm home. Tell me now, or I'm hanging up and pretending we never had this conversation." Scott kept his voice even, making sure there was no room to misunderstand his threat.

Zach sighed. "Here's the deal. You already know no one else is siding with him."

No one ever sided with Hank's calls to fire him, so why was Scott's gut churning?

"But a couple of the other board members are tired of this back and forth between the two of you, so they've got a proposal that's meant to put an end to it." Zach emphasized the words. "All you have to do is play along, and then they can tell Cartee you're not a liability, and everyone can move on with their lives."

Scott's eyes narrowed. "Why are you over-explaining yourself?"

"We have to bring in someone to fix your public image."

"What? No." Scott's voice rose in volume, irritation searing through him. They wanted to do a publicity makeover on him? "I'm not letting some uptight asshole teach me how to act in public. I left that life behind for a reason. No. Fucking. Way."

"Listen." Zach's voice softened for the first time since he'd called. "I know. I'd say I'm sorry, but you brought this on yourself. You already know this shit, so play nice until it's over, and we'll be all right."

"Whatever." He had no intention of doing so.

"Promise me you'll at least pretend you're going along with this for whomever we hire." A hint of pleading wove into Zach's voice.

"Yeah, I promise." Scott disconnected the call without further formality. He slammed the side of his fist against the steering wheel, biting back a scream of frustration. The one thing in the entire world that could send his aggravation soaring was someone telling him how to do his job.

When his parents had divorced almost a decade ago, he'd jumped on the chance to break away from exactly that. It was the perfect opportunity to cash out his college fund, which gave him the spring board he needed to finally get his company off the ground and prove to investors he was worth their time. It had also meant for the first time in his life his father didn't own a controlling share of his social and public presence.

And now he was going to have a board-appointed shadow stepping in to play that role of *say what people want to hear, not what you want to say.* Fuck.

chapter three

Kenzie stepped off the silent elevator. A wall of glass stared back at her, the frosted name RINSLET telling her she was in the right place. A black-lacquered desk was visible from the hallway, and the leather chairs and coffee table in the front lobby of the office matched.

The girl behind the desk looked up and smiled as Kenzie approached. The receptionist was a stark contrast to her surroundings, in jeans and a baggy tee that hid any figure she might have had. "Good morning, can I help you?"

Kenzie didn't know what to think of the place, but she kept her confusion off her face. "I'm Mackenzie Carter, I have an eleven a.m. appointment with Mr. Johnston and Mr. McAllister."

"Of course." The brunette gestured toward the seats. "Someone should be right with you."

Kenzie perched on the edge of one of the overstuffed chairs, not wanting to sink in and have her pencil skirt slide up. The personalized snippets of her presentation skipped through her thoughts. She had printouts in her bag in case she needed paper visuals, her laptop was ready to hook up to a projector if they had one, and she knew her pitch backward and forward.

She crossed her legs and drummed her fingers on her knees, letting her attention trip around the room. Not that there was much to see. Prints that were mostly primary colors hung in black squares on white walls. The screaming coming from somewhere deep within the office was interesting. She wasn't sure if it was cheering or cussing. Or both.

A movement caught her attention. A glimpse of brown, spiked hair as someone rounded the corner, walking backward, attention on a short blonde keeping him company. It couldn't be him. There were a lot of well-built guys with brown hair. Her fingertips and lips pulsed with unformed memories from Saturday. There was no way. Why would coffee-shop guy be here?

He turned, and her stomach flipped. It was Mr. G4M3G0D himself. She had to clench her jaw to keep it from dropping open. He'd tossed a sport jacket and black tie over his T-shirt—his version of dressing up maybe?—and he wore it better than should be legal.

His eyes met hers, and she pasted a smile in place. He raised an eyebrow and took a step toward her.

The petite blonde—she had to be at least a foot shorter than him—grabbed his arm and spun him away. The woman wrapped her arms around his neck. He returned the hug, lifting her off the ground. When he put her down, she gave him a quick peck on the cheek and then whispered something in his ear.

Kenzie would have felt awkward spying on the

intimate moment if ambivalence weren't racing through her veins. So much for fantasies of picking up where they'd left off when she returned his jacket. Guilt smattered her disappointment. She shouldn't even be wishing for another morning with someone else's guy, but that didn't stop her imagination from teasing her.

"Ms. Carter?" A deep baritone startled her, and she spun to face a man who must have come from the other side of the office. "I'm Zach Johnston. Thanks for making time for us this morning."

She stood to shake his hand. He wore a pressed Oxford and beige slacks, and even made the ponytail of pale hair at the base of his neck look slick. He radiated composed and car salesman. But not used cars, she'd give him that much. Only high-end ones.

She took his offered hand, impressed at the firm, but not aggressive, handshake and warm grip. "Not a problem, Mr. Johnston." She made sure her smile was genuine. "I just hope I can help."

"Call me Zach, or this is going to get old fast." His expression stayed pleasant. "Scott." He only half turned away from her to angle himself toward coffee-shop guy.

Getting no response, he frowned and turned completely toward Mr. G4M3G0D. "Scott," he said louder. "Are you two done?"

Mr. G4M3G0D pulled his attention from the petite blonde the second time Zach called his name.

"My fault." The shorter woman broke away from Scott. She flashed Kenzie an apologetic smile, squeezed Zach's hand and gave him a kiss on the cheek, and then made her way toward the elevator.

Kenzie's gut sank. This was her potential client? The guy who made his jacket-covered, Linux T-shirt look like something that belonged in a *GQ* photo shoot? The gorgeous stranger who had haunted her thoughts all weekend?

"This is Ms. Carter," Zach introduced them.

"Kenzie, please." She extended her hand. His grip was firmer than she remembered, sending a pleasant tremor through her. She pushed the thought aside. This was business, he was probably attached, and that had been a one-time thing. Or really not even a thing.

"Beautiful name." Scott's smirk was the same as she remembered. "Shall we?" He stepped aside and gestured.

If he was going to pretend it had never happened, she could do the same. Whether or not she wanted to shake the frigid shell, a potential client wasn't the right place to do it.

They led her toward a conference room, once again with a glass wall, leaving it fully exposed to the world. A round table sat in the center of the room, and there was barely enough space for the four chairs around it. The seats were like almost everything else in the office so far: black, overstuffed, and straight out of a catalog.

Scott gestured to one. "Have a seat."

She sat across from them, mentally summoning the appropriate version of her pitch for the intimate setting and planning marketing and media visuals to pluck from her bag when the time was right. She told her nervous energy to stop, that this was just any other presentation. But it wasn't listening.

She exchanged a few more pleasantries and then dove into her pitch. The impassive faces staring back at her were unnerving, but she'd been through it before. Potential clients who thought they had the perfect poker face and wouldn't let on whether or not they were impressed until all was said and done.

She explained who her clients were, some of the better-known executives she'd worked with, everything she knew from heart but could make sound enthusiastic and genuine.

And then Scott laid his arms on the table and dropped his forehead on top.

Zach elbowed him.

Scott jerked upright again, one eyebrow raised, and slumped back in his seat.

Kenzie clenched her jaw but kept talking. Part of her wanted to walk out right then. There was no way she was getting—or wanted—this contract, but pride wouldn't let her give up. She had to at least put on a good show.

"Blah, blah, blah."

That was all Scott heard. He watched her talk, pink-glossed lips accentuating every word with perfection. He struggled to keep his expression neutral as his thoughts drifted to what she could do with those amazing lips.

Like every other person they'd seen that morning, she was reciting a bunch of meaningless tripe that only made sense if someone wasn't paying attention.

Which, at that point, he was trying not to do.

She looked good, though. Her suit highlighted every curve at least as well as her jeans had. He could still feel her slender figure under his hands. Hear her breathing, her gasps. He blinked and shook his head, forcing the memories away, and tried to focus on the presentation again.

But it wasn't as much fun as the fantasies. This professional version of her was everything he'd been afraid she was before they'd talked. He dropped his head into his arms.

Zach elbowed him sharply.

Scott rolled his eyes, leaned back in his chair instead, arms crossed, and exhaled. "Is there a reason you haven't kicked this one out yet?" he whispered.

"I'm sorry, is there a problem, gentlemen?" Ice lined Kenzie's question.

Zach's lips drew into a thin line.

"Not at all. I was hoping you could answer a question for me." Scott gave her his biggest grin.

Her smile didn't look as happy. "Of course."

He'd asked everyone else the same thing and had yet to get a satisfactory answer. "Tell me something about your company we can't get off the website."

She paused, her fingers twitched on the table, and then her smile slid back into place, and her blue eyes locked on his. "We go above and beyond to get the job done. We can make even the most dysfunctional couple look like happily-ever-after to the press, if that's what's required."

Scott blinked. He hadn't been expecting that. She didn't mean him and her, right? Talk about conflict of interest. His eyes never left Kenzie's.

"Good to know, but not what we're looking for. I'm sure you saw that when you prepped, and I can tell you're well-prepared."

A hint of pink crept over her face, and her cheeks relaxed, smile becoming more genuine.

So the person he remembered was still in there under the ice. The right compliment could win the professional her over. "Let's try this again. What can your company do for us? What, out of this vast sea of boredom that is destined to be the rest of my day, do you bring to the table that no one else does?"

"Me." There was no hesitation in her reply.

Good point. She was exactly what he wanted.

"Excuse us." Zach grabbed Scott by the arm and yanked him into the hallway. "What's the deal with her?"

"We like the same kind of coffee."

Zach shook his head and tugged on the door, latching it shut. "Did you meet her at The Roasting Company or something?"

"Yup." Scott let more of the memories tickle his thoughts. "But that's not the point. It doesn't matter that she's hot. Whatever happened was two days ago and completely irrelevant."

"So something did happen. That's why she's been half glaring at you, half swooning, since she walked in."

Had she been swooning? Scott grinned. "Maybe."

Zach exhaled loudly and rolled his eyes. "Swear to me you won't use whatever it was as an excuse to make this entire thing not work."

Scott was tired of the badgering. Not that he had

any intention of cooperating with anyone they brought on. "You're not honestly thinking of hiring her, are you?"

Zach smirked. "She's exactly what you need."

Scott bit back a growl. "I almost slept with her."

"*Almost* isn't worth anything. You'll find an excuse for every single person we bring in. At least her, you talk to. She came highly recommended, and it's obvious she's good at what she does."

Scott rolled his eyes, but he wasn't as disappointed as he expected to be. At least she'd be a fun distraction, and maybe he could get her to forget work long enough to finish what they started. He kept his creeping excitement from his voice. "Fine."

Zach was already heading back down the hall. "Let her know. I'll cancel the other appointments. We've got better things to do."

Scott couldn't hide his pleasure as he slipped back into the room and took the seat across from Kenzie. "Sorry about that."

"No problem." Her demeanor didn't give anything away.

That sucked; he was going to have to change that. Professional and prepared was one thing, but unyielding was completely unacceptable. Maybe acknowledging the elephant in the room would help. Besides, if he couldn't make her smile genuine... He wanted to see that flush again.

He leaned in, hands clasped and resting on the table, and voice low but distinct. "Saturday was killer, and I'm sorry I had to cut things short."

Her brow creased, voice flat. "Of course."

So much for breaking the ice. He leaned back. "I see. Am I the only one who enjoyed myself?"

A waver disrupted her stern tone. "Mr. McAllister—"

"Scott," he corrected her.

She barely paused. "As far as this presentation is concerned, those two people in that coffee shop are not the same as the two people sitting here. Or at least one of them isn't. If you're not interested in my services—my publicity experience—then I'm not sure why you're wasting my time."

Still not afraid to speak her mind. Still absolutely intriguing. "I never said I wasn't interested."

"No, but your demeanor through the entire meeting did. I'm not surprised you're looking for outside help, but you're going to have to be ready to change before it will do you any good."

There was nothing to change, but the conversation would be over if he told her that, and he wasn't ready for it to end. "And you're the person who could help me do that if I were to admit I had a problem?"

"I could be. As long as you understand if anyone were to think you hired me because of what may or may not have happened between those two people who weren't us, it would devastate my career. I'm not interested in that."

Wow, she was tough. That was sexy. And mildly irritating. "So no kissing and telling. I can do that."

"You've already told your business partner."

He glanced behind him at the closed door.

"Zach doesn't count, he knows everything about me. And apparently he thinks that gives him license to choose my keeper for the next few months. The job is yours if you're not afraid of the challenge." He couldn't help slipping the last line in. Something told him she was exactly the opposite of afraid of challenge. That she'd jump on the chance.

Her mouth twisted in thought. "I'm in on one condition."

Damn that was a good look for her. "I assume there will be several conditions. Put it in the contract and we'll negotiate."

"You may not want this in the contract." She brushed an invisible strand of hair from her face. "The blonde in the lobby—your girlfriend or his?"

He studied her, curious about the question. "You're jealous?"

Her flush grew. "Hardly. I understand you're doing this for business reasons, but frequently that intersects with people's personal lives. I don't care what you do in your spare time as long as you keep it out of the news, but if you're dating someone who doesn't know how fast and loose you play with other women, I need to know if that has to be spun in a positive light when she finds out and dumps you."

Wow, okay, he hadn't expected that. He bit back a chuckle when he realized she was serious. He'd wanted to make the conversation more pleasant, not less so. "First of all, fast and loose? You approached me. Second, I'm two hundred percent single." He drummed his fingers on the table. "Rae's not my girlfriend, she's Zach's fiancée. We're close, but I swear on my next game not crashing and burning at release that we're just friends."

She tilted her head to the side, studying him for a moment. It accentuated her neck. Soft, kissable … yeah, this was going to be fun.

"All right. You'll have the contract this afternoon. As soon as it's signed, we can talk," she said.

He couldn't hide his grin as he stood. "Looking forward to it." Keeping his investors happy, being able to skirt their lame-ass edict, he was definitely looking forward to it.

chapter four

Had it really only been twenty-four hours since her sales pitch? At least Scott had been serious about bringing her on fast. And she still couldn't believe he'd hired her in the first place. Her company had sent the contract over before lunch the day before, and he'd signed and returned it early enough to insist she start on Tuesday.

And here she was. Kenzie smiled at the receptionist as she approached the front desk. Her stomach was doing somersaults at being back in their offices, memories of the weekend before still teasing her. But work was work. "Is Mr. McAllister in?" She'd seen his SUV in the parking lot—part of the reason her imagination was running wild—but there was no reason to let anyone else know that.

"I'll tell you one more time. Call me Scott." He strode around the corner, pausing with an eyebrow raised when he saw her.

The way his gaze raked over her sent a rush of anticipation through her veins. She clenched her jaw, trying and failing to ignore the reaction.

A crooked smile played on his face before vanishing, and he brushed past her. "You're here for the day, correct?"

He was walking away from her? She spun and followed him toward the elevator, letting the confusion show in her voice "Yes."

"Nothing important or outstanding vying for your attention?"

"Only if you consider getting to know you important." She stared at his back.

"I hear it is sometimes." He pushed the down button. "That means I can get some actual work done. Are you coming?"

"I, uh…" She stepped into the elevator with him, not sure what to make of the abrupt attitude. "Apparently."

He was wearing jeans and a Hulk T-shirt. He glanced at her, and then went back to staring at the blips of light counting down floors as they descended. "I told you, casual office environment."

"This is what I wear to work. You're going to have to learn to do the same." The fragmented conversation made her stumble, but she wasn't going to let him take verbal control.

"I doubt I'd wear the skirt as well as you. What are the odds you have sneakers in your car?"

"Pretty good." Or at least she'd regain control as soon as she figured out what they were talking about. They stepped into the parking garage she'd left only moments earlier. "I suspect you already know this, but we're moving away from your office."

"Grab them."

She bit back a snarl at the order, and took her time strolling two rows over to her car to grab her running shoes. What had happened to the man who didn't seem capable of taking anything seriously?

He waited by his SUV, patiently holding her door, not saying anything else until they were both inside. "We only have a couple more hours of good light. After eleven or twelve, it turns to shit."

Maybe he was actually going to try and make this publicity thing work. The language was going to have to go. She made a mental note. "The lighting where?"

Harsh sun assaulted her when they pulled into morning traffic, and she dropped her sunglasses into place. Within a couple of minutes he had maneuvered them out of the downtown pack of cars, and they were heading in the opposite direction of the last of the straggling commuters.

"The beach." He merged onto the interstate, heading west toward the airport. "You can play twenty questions with me along the way."

None of this information was helping. "I'm not dressed for the beach because, even if I wasn't expecting to be in an office today, we're in Salt Lake. No beaches."

His expression cracked, and he laughed. "Sorry, I can't keep a straight face any more. This whole *I'm too important and busy to be polite* thing doesn't do it for me. How do you even pull that off? Is it like a switch—on is flirty and fun Kenzie, and off is carrying the weight of the world in her laptop bag?"

The question dug deeper than she wanted to admit, mingling with the accusations of Riley's she still hadn't been able to forget. At least he hadn't called her frigid. She flopped her head back against the seat and exhaled. "It's not a switch, but the situation is different now. Why are we going to the…beach?"

He kept his attention on the road, still grinning. "Okay, I'll concede there are no crashing waves, and you probably don't want the sand between your toes, but it's a lake, and I think that means the land around it qualifies as a beach. I'm drafting out a location in a game, and I need pictures, visuals, and a hands-on experience."

At least he hadn't pushed the other issue. "That doesn't sound like an executive's job. Why don't you have someone else do it?"

He spared her a glance, brows raised in disbelief. "For the same reason I do game testing. If I surrender my favorite parts of work just because someone sticks a nameplate and a title on my office door, what's the point of being in charge?"

"Oh." She didn't have a comeback. Instead, she watched the scenery shift and change as they headed past the mountains and into another valley. They left the traffic behind, following the twisting interstate.

A large building loomed into sight as they approached their destination. She recognized Saltair—it looked like a castle from Arabian Nights. If Disney had animated it. And then left it on the back lot to collect dust. "I haven't been out here since I was in high school. The Foo Fighters I think."

He pulled onto the dirt shoulder outside the chain-link fence surrounding the building. Once upon a time the spot had been a tourist venue. Now it was only used for concerts, meaning the rest of the time the entire area was abandoned. No one had much interest in playing on a beach that was more sagebrush than sand, or in a lake filled with salt and brine shrimp.

He turned to her. "I was at that show. You don't really strike me as a mosh pit kind of girl."

Even just thinking about being jostled like that gave her a headache. "I'm not. We were in the balcony. Amazing concert, though. So much energy."

He grabbed a duffel bag from the back seat of the SUV. Oh, the things she'd imagined doing back there. Heat rushed through Kenzie, and the way his gaze raked over her made it difficult to ignore.

He turned away and pushed his door open. "You might want to leave your jacket in the car. And your shoes."

She paused with one sleeve down her arm. Why had she worn a sleeveless shirt that morning? Sand on her dry clean only jacket, or sun on her bare arms? Why was she even debating? She took off the jacket. "Do you have some place I can hang it?"

He started to say something and then shook his head. His hands brushed hers and lingered a few seconds when he took the jacket, sending a pleasant chill across her skin. He hopped out of the car, opened the back door, and hung her top from a hook before closing everything up again.

A few seconds later, her door swung open. He was on the other side, holding out his hand. "Coming?"

She accepted the offer, his rough palm gentle against hers, and landed in the dirt next to him. A cloud of dust floated around her feet, and she sighed. The rocks would be murder on her heels. She grabbed her sneakers and dropped them on the ground. She slipped out of one heel and dipped her toes into the running shoe. As she started to tilt, she realized she was rapidly losing her balance.

"Watch it." His arm wrapped around her waist.

Her hand flew to his shoulder out of instinct. His sturdy grip was hot and enticing, holding her up, and he smelled faintly of aftershave. Sunlight warmed her cheeks, and for a moment all she felt was him pressed against her.

She swallowed and straightened up. "Sorry, I'm not usually a klutz."

"No worries." His voice was thick. His hand lingered on her hip.

She used him for balance—at least that's what she tried to tell herself—reluctantly pulling away when she finished changing her shoes. Sneakers, stockings, and a sleeveless silk blouse; she was glad no one else could see how ridiculous she looked. "I still don't know what we're doing."

He headed toward the water, talking over his shoulder. "I'm working. I assume you're trying to find out why I'm a fuckup and planning to tell me how to fix it."

Her brow furrowed, and she quickened her pace to keep up with him. So much for him being a willing participant. "Then tell me about yourself."

He stopped several yards back from the water and dropped his duffel bag on the sand. Maybe sand wasn't the right word. It was gritty, but unrecognizable patches of green and brown dotted the entire landscape. "I like long walks on the beach, the company of a gorgeous woman who can hold her own in a conversation, and hot wax. Or candles, something like that."

Candle wax? She inhaled sharply through clenched teeth, momentarily distracted. "Not what I meant."

He pulled a camera and lens from the bag and hooked them together. The screen on the back of the camera flickered on, reflecting a miniature version of the lake. "Then you should have asked what you meant." There was no irritation in his voice. He moved closer to her, arm brushing hers, and held the camera in front of her. "What do you see?"

It took focus not to lean into the contact. "A lot of water?" She didn't know what she was supposed to be seeing. Other states had scenic lake fronts, but this was just a bunch of gray and blue that stretched into haze.

She made a conscious effort not to rest her head against his shoulder. They were working. "What did you do—not what's in the information you sent me—that pissed off this board member of yours?"

He pursed his lips and angled toward the island in the distance. He snapped a few shots before shifting position again. "A lot of water. Nice." He changed the view screen so it displayed one of the shots he'd just taken and showed it to her.

He'd captured an angle of Saltair so the clouds drifted behind and around it, the sunlight striking the gold towers and gleaming, making the entire thing look like it was surrounded by mist and on fire. It was just a trick of light, but it was amazing. She looked between the building and the photo. "How did you do that?"

He shrugged, shouldered the bag, and started walking again, camera hanging from a strap around his wrist. "It's all about perspective. His last wife—number three maybe—tried to pick me up at a party a couple of years ago."

Why didn't the casual way he confessed surprise her? "A couple of years?" She gazed at their surroundings as they strolled along the sand. In the distance, a pair of gutted and vandalized buildings loomed against an otherwise barren landscape. "Were you working with him then?"

"Nope. He bought in about a year later."

"So what makes you think he still holds it against you?" The arrogance was both intriguing and confounding. "You can't be the only guy she did that with. And if he blamed you for the breakup, why would he invest in your company?"

Scott glanced at her, a small smile playing on his face. "Yeah, he does. You should see some of the shit he puts me through while trying to hold my job over my head. This bullshit with you is just another hoop to jump through."

She was a bullshit hoop? The words dug deeper than she expected. Still, she could spin it to her advantage. If he needed her around, she wasn't going to be the one to beg. It was his dime. She stopped. "I don't have to be here. This isn't going to work anyway if you're not going to try."

"What?" He spun, already several steps ahead of her. "That's not what I meant."

"It is." She crossed her arms. "You pretended to fall asleep during my presentation, and you've dodged every attempt I've made to do my job this morning."

He clenched his jaw. "Because I'm difficult and need fixing. Isn't that why I hired you?"

"It's certainly a convenient excuse." She turned away. "I'll be in the car, doing work for people who want me to be working. Find me when you're done traipsing through the sand."

"Kenzie." His call hit her back.

She kept walking, irritation pumping through her. It wasn't hurt. Not even close. She didn't care if he thought little to nothing of her job, as long as he let her do it. The non-ache grew as she reached the SUV and realized he still hadn't stopped her.

"Wait." His hand wrapped loosely around her arm.

The contact sent a pleasant jolt through her, one she didn't want to be feeling. She closed her eyes and inhaled sharply.

He let go abruptly. "I didn't mean to be insulting."

His sincerity was salve in wounds she didn't want to acknowledge. Contrite was exactly what she needed, and she had to push her advantage. She spun back to face him. "That's what we'll start with. You need to learn to think before you speak."

He shrugged. "I always think. I just don't expect people to take it so personally."

Of course. She blew a loose strand of hair out of her face.

He watched her silently, brown eyes wide and pleading.

Damn that look. "Okay, we'll try again. You have to work with me, though." She locked her gaze on him, trying to convey how serious she was.

He separated his camera and lens, and nestled both back in their bag. "Then you have to do the same."

She scowled. "That's kind of what I do. Like it's my entire job."

He traced a finger down her arm. "All right, we'll talk. You can assault me with questions to figure out how to manipulate me, and I can use metaphor and obtuse examples to subconsciously convince you I'm perfect as is."

His touch was enticing, and a warm tremor ran through her. That sounded fantastic. And counterproductive to her job. "That's not cooperating."

He winked at her. "You won't know any better if I do it right."

Her tentative grip on the situation was slipping. "That's not how this works." Gawd he was so infuriating. And fascinating. How did he get away with it? The easy way he ignored convention and slid into whatever he wanted regardless of what was appropriate.

He tucked a strand of hair behind her ear. "Your hair looks gorgeous in this light. It catches the golds just right."

His compliment warmed her further, and she mentally told her pleased reaction to calm down. "This isn't helping me do my job."

He tilted his head to the side, the corner of his mouth pulled into a disarming half-smile, and his brown eyes raked over her face. It took him a moment to answer. "Me neither." He clicked the locks off on his SUV and stepped around her to open the back door. "Come on."

She could tell he had a plan—that he wasn't just flitting from one thought to the next without direction—but damned if she could figure out what it was. The ordered part of her loathed it. The part of her that wanted to be more reckless was fascinated to watch him work. "We're leaving? That didn't take long."

He slammed the door shut and locked the car again. He stepped next to her and nodded toward the buildings in the distance. "Not unless you're really miserable. That's what I'm actually here for." He held up a folded blanket, the navy fleece absorbing the sunlight. "But I need to take a lot of pictures. This is so you have a place to sit without getting your skirt dirty."

Her cheeks warmed at the consideration, and as she studied the graffitied walls in the near distance, her blood warmed with other thoughts. It was a shame she couldn't practice being non-frigid now. An abandoned spot out in the open but with no one around for miles except distant freeway traffic? The memories of his hands on her skin, his fingers pulling her hair, were all enough to send her thoughts into overdrive.

He glanced over his shoulder. "You coming?"

It didn't take much self-control, but it did fill her with regret to bite back the answer of *not yet, but I'm hoping to soon* that she would have given him on Saturday. Instead, she forced out a simple, "Sure."

chapter five

The inside of the abandoned barely-a-building was exactly what Scott had been hoping for when he'd seen the outside from the freeway a few weeks back. The only things still standing were the cinder block walls. Two-by-fours and other debris littered the ground, morning light streamed through the non-existent ceiling, and decades of spray paint decorated all of it. It was the perfect inspiration for the room he was designing in-game.

And he was having a hard time focusing on anything but the gorgeous scenery in the middle of the devastation. The curve of her ass in her pencil skirt. The way the fabric slid several inches up her thighs when she lowered herself onto the blanket he'd set out for her. The fantastic view when the top of her shirt pulled open, exposing a hint of smooth flesh and round breasts.

A throb below his waist nagged him, and he adjusted his jeans. That was the last thing he needed her to see. Or the first. He shoved the thoughts aside and tried to focus on taking reference shots while she talked.

And maybe a couple of her.

She stared up at his viewfinder, lips pursed, but a smile danced behind her eyes. "I'm not your subject matter."

He shrugged and turned back to the building interior. It was probably for the best; he really needed these pictures.

"Your calendar says you have an investor dinner in a couple of weeks. That sounds big." She had been poring over his social engagements for the last fifteen minutes, figuring out what she thought it was appropriate to prep him for and looking for opportunities to make him shine for the right people.

Just like his dad had forced him into when he was younger. So unappealing. But at least she was kind about it instead of degrading. He snapped a couple more shots. "We do it every year. Buy expensive food for the people who make sure we stay in business, present slide shows, assure them we're not washing their money down the drain—funny how few of them ask how much the night costs—and play nice for four or so hours."

He knew they were a necessary evil, but he still hated knowing that almost everyone he spoke to during an investor dinner only saw dollar signs when they looked at him. It might be nice instead if they actually cared what kind of work and creativity went into the projects he and his teams produced.

"Perfect." She set her phone on her knee, tapping away. "This is one of those opportunities that we can take advantage of, spread some good will, remind people how affable you are." She leaned over farther, hair falling around her face before she tucked it behind one ear, bottom lip resting between her teeth in concentration.

His breath caught, and he let his gaze linger. He pulled his attention away again when she looked up, but not before her eyes met his and he glimpsed the pink spreading over her cheeks.

"What are you wearing?" she asked.

How had that become an issue? He looked down, and an upside-down Hulk glared back at him. "Come on, you can't make me change my everyday clothes. This is what I wear to the office."

She exhaled. "I meant to the dinner. You've rented a tux, correct?"

Oh. That. *Rented.* He almost snorted at the word. He'd had one tailored for him by a brilliant designer he knew in Italy. "No."

"Another thing for the list."

He tucked his camera into its bag, set it all aside, and crouched in front of her, hand covering hers before she could tap out more notes. It took concentration not to stroke his finger over the fleshy edge of her palm. "Please don't." He kept his voice kind but firm. "I already own one."

"You own a tux." She didn't yank her hand away. It took a moment before she moved it to make more notes. "If you show up in blue polyester, I'm quitting."

He was surprised she hadn't walked out the door that morning, and he was taking it as a good sign. "It's black. I'm not a formal-affair virgin."

Her flush grew, but she didn't rise to the bait. "Right. What else?"

He didn't want to be having this conversation. Time for a new one. "Why did you do it?" He left the question intentionally vague. He rested his elbows on his knees, still studying her.

She tore her attention from her phone, staring back in confusion. "Do…?"

"Saturday. I see you in there almost every weekend, always alone, and I assume you've seen me too since you knew which car was mine. What made you approach me this one time?"

The pink flushing her cheeks darkened, but she didn't look away. "Not that I know what you're talking about, but if I did, it was only because I needed a place to sit."

Ouch, that stung. "Right, that wasn't you because of conflict of interest. So this other woman, who you're intimately acquainted with and I'd like to be, didn't just pick an empty slice of wall to lean against like she normally does because…"

Her lips drew into a thin line. "This conversation is counterproductive."

It was completely productive if it distracted her from telling him how to dress—and maybe helped him figure out how to get her undressed. "I disagree."

"Which is why you hired me instead of doing your own publicity."

He wouldn't be deterred, but he also knew better than to tell her that wasn't exactly why he'd hired her. "You—sorry, she—was just looking for a little conversation that morning?"

Her eyes narrowed and she blew a strand of hair off her forehead. "Will you drop this if I tell you?"

Headway, perfect. "Maybe. If I think you're telling the truth and not just making something up to get rid of me."

She clenched her teeth, hesitating.

He didn't interrupt.

"Fine." She exhaled. "I had something to prove."

That was interesting. "To whom?"

She paused again. "Myself."

She wasn't telling him everything. Interesting. "Did it work?"

Her brow furrowed, and she chewed her bottom lip.

He wanted to be doing that.

She twirled a strand of hair around her finger. "It might have worked better if … no, you know what? It worked fantastically. I found out what I needed to know. Yup, it's all good. What else is on your calendar in the next few weeks?"

The way she had set her phone aside and leaned forward, bringing her face closer to his, told him she wasn't shutting him out. He was close to something. "Soon, I promise. I'm still curious about this proving something to yourself idea. What, exactly?"

Her breath hitched, and she licked her lips, eyes pulling away from his. "You said you'd drop it."

"There were conditions." He sat cross-legged across from her on the blanket, keeping less than an inch between her knees and his. "But I won't push it if you don't want to talk about it. My schedule, then?"

She still wouldn't look at him, and the corner of her mouth twitched with something he couldn't identify. Her voice was soft when she finally replied. "I had an argument with my sister that morning. She called me a lot of names, I probably called her some back, and you seemed like a good way to prove her wrong.”

He leaned forward, intrigued. “It’s not often a woman admits to using me.” It wasn’t an unfamiliar concept, they just usually didn’t outright tell him that’s what they were doing.

She ducked her head. “Sorry.”

“Don’t be.” He traced a finger over her knee, her heat seeping through the texture of her stockings. “Do I get more details than that?”

She finally looked at him, indecision dancing behind her eyes. A smile pushed away some of her embarrassment. “I suppose I owe you that much. Funny, given the things we talked about that day, how this one little admission embarrasses me.”

He abandoned thoughts of trying to work. The casual flow of the conversation had his blood racing. He let his gaze linger on her moist lips, sharp memories of how she tasted taunting him.

“She called me frigid,” Kenzie finally blurted out. “I’d seen you in there so many times before and yeah, okay, you’re attractive, I admit it. So I struck up a conversation with you to prove I wasn’t uptight.”

He was used to people complimenting if they wanted a favor, but something about the fact the words had come from her settled deep inside, warming him more than the sun creeping through the roofless rafters overhead.

He’d already asked once, but wanted to see if she’d be more forthcoming. “Did it work? Did you prove it?”

She traced a finger along her collar, drawing his

eyes down as she played with her top shirt button. He shifted his position when his cock throbbed in response, and his imagination taunted him with images of her undoing each button slowly while he watched.

She swallowed. "Not as thoroughly as I would have liked."

His arousal screamed in response to the teasing. The possible opportunity to finish what they'd started. He forced his voice to remain steady. "So I know I'm just some boring executive and not the mysterious guy with the love van you thought I was, but I'm available if you're still interested."

She shook her head and leaned back on both hands, shoulders stretched back and full breasts jutting toward him. Amusement and uncertainty warred for her expression. "You're not paying me to sleep with you."

Ouch. Dangerous territory. "It's true. But I'm also paying you a fixed fee, not hourly. So if I decided we were done for the day, any free time you had would be yours to do what or whomever you pleased."

She extended her legs in front of her, crossing them at the ankles. "It's not professional."

He loved this banter with her. The way she let him poke and prod at the conversation. "It's not supposed to be. You're proving you're not uptight."

She sat back up, pulling her legs in and tucking them to the side, hair falling around her face. "It's a conflict of interest."

Every time he thought she was going to tell him no—slap him and put a stop to the entire thing—she set out another tease. Was she doing it intentionally? He had to prod a little more. The heaving chest taunting him was too tempting. "Not necessarily. Not if it's purely physical, right? No emotional attachment. I promise it won't get in the way of work, you promise the same, and then we're just two people playing outside of business hours, right?"

She shifted on the blanket, pushing to her knees and crawling closer until her nose was inches from his. "You're really good at this negotiation stuff."

He usually sucked at it. He was too straightforward for most people. He said what he wanted; they either said no or yes. "Honestly? You're just really tempting motivation. Work's done for the day. Are you interested in something extra-curricular?"

She trailed her fingers down his arm, nails brushing his knuckles. He bit back a groan at the light touch. Her voice was soft, but her eyes never left his when she said, "Definitely."

He flipped his hand, loosely grasping her wrist and eliciting a gasp. Her skin was hot against his. He raised her fingers to his mouth, kissing each fingertip before moving to her palm and then her inner wrist. The faint flower of her perfume made his head swim, and her pulse against his lips was intoxicating.

His gaze met hers, and she gave him a shy smile. "Shouldn't we go somewhere more private?"

He continued to kiss along her palm, replying between each peck. "If you'd prefer. But there's no one around, so I don't know if *more private* exists."

Kenzie shook her head and gave a small laugh. "You've got a point."

Scott raised an eyebrow and gave her a crooked smile. "Too easy." He might have been tempted to counter the obvious innuendo, but exploring more of the woman in front of him was far more appealing. He let go of her hand and shifted his weight to his knees. Crawling forward, he stopped when his nose was just inches from hers.

She sighed and tilted toward him. "But I'm not. That's what this is about."

He dipped his head toward her neck, mouth hovering millimeters from her skin but never touching it as he slid his lips up. His voice was low. "No, it's not."

She sighed and arched her back, pressing closer to the feather-light tease. "What's it about, then?" she asked breathily.

His blood pressure screamed in response to the sensual movement, cock straining against his jeans. He brushed the outside edge of her ear, and she whimpered. Geez, that noise was enough to screw with a guy's head. He whispered, "It's about us, and how intensely I'd like to ravish you."

Her light laugh faded into a moan when he traced his tongue up the curve of her neck. She rested her arms on the ground to support her weight and stretched her legs out next to his. "You really have a way with words."

"I have a way with other things too." He grazed his teeth over her earlobe, her jaw, her lower lip, before finally pressing his lips to hers. He growled against her mouth when she returned the kiss, hungry. It was even more intense than he remembered, and very not uptight. Her tongue danced around his, searching, massaging.

He rested a hand at the base of her neck. Her skin was soft against his palm, filling his thoughts with images of what the rest of her felt like. Lust and desire obliterated any other thoughts. She pressed forward, warm chest molding against his, breasts rubbing through their shirts. Some of that clothing needed to go soon.

She traced her nails over his collarbone before resting her hand on his jaw. She gasped when they broke apart, running her tongue over her bottom lip, studying him with a need he knew reflected his own.

"If you're bragging, I'm going to need proof." Her cheeks tinged with the timid taunt, and she ducked her head.

Damn it this was fun. He tangled his fingers in her hair and tugged her head back so he could look her in the eye. His voice was thick with want. "Happy to oblige."

He traced his mouth down her throat, her whimpers vibrating against his lips. She dropped her hand to his waist and pushed up the bottom of his T-shirt. He inhaled sharply at the skin-on-skin contact. Resting his other hand at the small of her back, he lowered her to the ground.

His fingers drew lines along her collarbone before dipping lower along the hint of cleavage taunting him. When she gasped and arched her back again, it spurred him on. He undid her top two buttons. White lace stretched against full breasts, and his body responded. He wouldn't have guessed it was possible for him to get any harder, and he would have been wrong.

She tugged his shirt, and he broke away from her long enough to let her pull it over his head. The warm morning air hit his back, and her smooth palms traced over his chest. The delicate touch was so different from what he was used to—an enticing combination of hesitation and confidence instead of assumption that he would perform because it was expected of him.

He kissed along the top of one breast, dipping into the valley between them before moving to the other. Each time she gasped, it made his pulse pound faster and spurred him on. He worked the flesh free from one cup, and her nails scraped over his back. He growled at the sensation, lowering his mouth to her already hard nipple. He alternated between flicking his tongue over the nub and nibbling lightly.

His cock strained against denim, protesting the barrier keeping it from what it really wanted. He moved a knee between hers, nudging her legs apart, never letting up his attentions on her chest. His other hand dropped to her thigh and pushed her skirt up.

He couldn't fight his smirk—or the loss of the last of the blood to his head—when he brushed the top of her stockings. "Thigh highs? That's just sexy."

Her flush deepened, though he wasn't sure anymore if it was from embarrassment or excitement, and she squirmed against him. "I'll keep that in mind."

He covered her mouth with his again, swallowing her moans as he pushed her skirt to her hips. He trailed his finger along the elastic hugging her hip, tracing a line down her skin toward the warmth between her legs.

She shifted to draw closer to his touch, and he obliged, pushing the crotch of her panties aside and brushing her slit. The slippery wet against his finger added another layer to his need, but he could hold out a little longer. He spread her lower lips, and she pushed against his hand, inhaling sharply.

He dipped lower, fingers hovering at the edge of her hole before gliding inside. Her cry of pleasure and the way she ground against him drove him wild. He pumped slowly inside her, thumb searching higher to find the swollen nub begging for attention. Her breathing grew jagged when he brushed her clit.

He let the sound of her gasps and sharp breaths drive his pace. She sucked in a breath and arched against him, clenching around his fingers as she came.

She draped her hands at the base of his neck and pulled him back for another breathless kiss. There was hesitation on her face when they broke apart.

He didn't know how to interpret the look. His brow furrowed in concern. "Is something wrong?"

She turned her gaze away, and she undid the button on his jeans. Her voice was quiet. "I want more. I want you."

He growled with lust and relief when she slid his zipper down and wrapped her fingers around his cock. It took some fumbling on his part, but he managed to pull a condom from his wallet, unwrap it, and roll it on.

He nudged her legs farther apart, bulbous head hovering at her opening. She scooted forward, and her moan mingled with his gasp when he drove deep inside her. He rocked slowly against her, trying to prolong the moment, but she increased the pace.

His laugh was strained. "I won't last long if you keep that up."

She pushed harder against him. "I'm not worried about it."

He couldn't hold back anymore. She was so wet and tight around him. He sought out her clit again, thumb bumping against it as he pounded hard and fast inside her. Her short breaths told him she was close to peaking again, and he struggled to hold out. She screamed when she came, muscles tightening around him and milking him.

He grunted and thrust harder, orgasm building inside and washing over him suddenly, draining him as he came.

Her rhythm slowed with him until they stopped, but his pulse was still hammering. He leaned over her, brushing a loose strand of hair from her forehead. "That was amazing. You're amazing."

She laughed nervously, bottom lip catching between her teeth.

He kissed her softly before rolling to the side and landing on his back on the blanket. He stared up at the sky through the lack of roof.

She curled up next to him, head resting on his shoulder and hand on his chest. Her breath tickled his skin when she spoke. "So that's what it's like to let loose a little."

He chuckled. It never had been before, but he sure as hell hoped it would be again. "No, that was better."

chapter six

Kenzie perched on the edge of the overstuffed easy chair, careful not to sink into it. Why did so many places think it was a good idea to have seats that swallowed their guests and were impossible to stand from gracefully?

Men in expensive suits milled like cattle in the lobby of the steakhouse, chatting with the hostess, with each other, with acquaintances they were far nicer to now than they would be once they parted ways. It used to bother her that these lunches truly were one of the last great bastions of the boys club—very few women joined their counterparts here—but she'd gotten used to it over time.

"Hey." Scott's greeting startled her.

His voice sent her pulse racing. Every time she thought about the day before, heat flooded her. She tried to hide her reaction by glancing at her watch before she acknowledged him. That had been physical, this was business. They had both agreed. She could do this.

Right?

He took a seat on the arm of her chair, and she resisted the urge to lean into him. Now wasn't the time, especially not in public. The trouble she'd get in if anyone knew she was intimate with a client— whether or not it was impacting her work. She scooted away, trying to mask it under the disguise of studying his wardrobe. He wore jeans with more holes than fabric and an Iron Maiden shirt that looked like he'd buffed his car with it.

The professional side of her climbed back into control. She pursed her lips. "What are you wearing?"

"Clothes." He stood and offered her a hand.

She bit back a sigh at the familiar touch, pulling away as soon as was polite.

A tiny frown crossed his face and then vanished again. "Thing about places like this, they tend to frown on nudity."

Places like this. One of the nicest restaurants in town. After spending hours the night before poring over Scott's past—which seemed to start abruptly nine years ago, and she hadn't figured out yet why he didn't have a childhood—she'd realized he really didn't have issues with the media or negative press except when it came to how he held himself professionally in public. Big surprise. He tended to offend people at trade shows, piss people off in interviews, and draw all the wrong crowds in hospitality suites.

She'd asked him to meet her here because the city's upper crust held their business lunches here. It was always a good place to point out how they behaved and see how her apprentice showed up without coaching so she knew how much work she had left to do.

Some of the other groups waiting for tables—she'd been told at least forty-five minutes, and these men who were supposedly on their lunch hour were mingling and waiting anyway—were glancing at them and frowning as they muttered to each other.

Maybe she should have at least warned him what kind of a place this was. Those jeans were horrible. It was a good thing there wasn't a dress code. But this was what she'd needed to see.

She forced her smile to remain pleasant. "They put my name on their list. I guess we have a little while to wait still."

Scott looked her over, dark eyes lingering on her face for a moment. The corner of his mouth pulled up. "Your hair still looks better down."

He turned away before she could reply, which was fine with her. It gave her a chance to hide the flush on her cheeks. She hadn't left it down for him. She just hadn't had time to pull it back that morning. She tucked a strand behind her ear and suppressed a growl when she realized he was making his way to the hostess' podium.

"Scott." She tried to keep her voice low, but threatening. "What are you doing?"

He glanced at her. "You really should have called ahead." He turned back to the brunette, who was studying her nails. "Becca, how's my favorite girl?" His greeting carried through the lobby, drawing more than a few nearby glances.

Kenzie resisted the urge to find a plant to hide behind. What was he doing?

"Hey, hon." Becca's demeanor shifted in an instant when she saw him. Her shoulders straightened, and she stopped leaning on the nearby wall. "Haven't seen you in a while. You look good."

Kenzie pursed her lips and watched the exchange in silence, realization dawning on her. He knew the woman, but how?

"You know how it goes." Scott leaned in on his arm and rested his weight on the podium. "My boss is an asshole slave driver."

Becca giggled—actually tittered and covered her mouth with her fingertips while Kenzie bit back a gag—and grabbed two menus from their hiding spot. "Your table is ready if you are."

"Always." Scott's smile was warm and genuine.

Amazement tempered Kenzie's inappropriate memories as she followed them through the crowded restaurant. He nodded, waved, or smiled at half the staff. Not only had he been there before, but he was on friendly terms with almost everyone. He was a little loud and under-dressed, but he seemed friendly enough. She still didn't understand why his board was complaining.

Their table was near the back, away from most of the din. Before taking his own seat, Scott held out her chair for her and scooted it in while she sat. She tried and failed to ignore the warmth in her chest at how flawlessly he'd done it.

Their waitress was with them within seconds, filling their water and setting a bread basket on the table.

"Tanya. New haircut? It looks good." Scott's voice was distinct, even in the chatter-filled room, drawing more glowers from around them.

That kind of attention was bad, and it pushed away some of the lingering lust. Kenzie didn't know if she should shush him or sink farther in her seat.

"Thanks." The redhead fluffed the short bob. "Got tired of the baby wrapping sticky fingers in it."

"At least she's outgrown the spitting up, right?" Scott asked.

"Totally." Tanya pulled a pad and pen from her apron pocket. "Getting milk puke out of these black button-downs is murder."

Someone nearby coughed, and voices died down, the entire section growing quiet. Kenzie grimaced at the mental image invoked by the conversation and the attention they were drawing.

"I'm going to take your word for it." Scott didn't look fazed. "Is the special any good?"

"Fresh prosciutto-wrapped chicken with roasted cauliflower. Dessert's a surprise."

Scott looked at Kenzie. "You're not vegetarian or anything like that, right? You like a good, thick slice of meat every once in a while?"

She should have seen that coming. Kenzie felt more heads turning in their direction, and the heat in her face grew. She took a long swallow of ice water, intentionally ignoring his second question. "I'm not vegetarian."

"Sweet. We'll both have the special, and the calamari to start."

Tanya looked at her. "Anything to drink?"

She'd have the strongest anything in the house if she thought she could get away with it. "A glass of the house white wine."

Scott raised an eyebrow, gaze lingering on her

as he spoke. "Coke for me."

"I'll be back soon," Tanya assured them.

Scott glanced at his phone as soon as she was gone. "It's noon. I'm already driving you to drink?"

Kenzie tried to keep her expression neutral. She wasn't going to let him get to her. "You're lecturing me on what is and isn't appropriate?"

He rolled his eyes. "I wouldn't dream of it. Some of us like people the way they are."

Had she wounded him? No, the sharp edge in his stare screamed challenge. She pushed back anything else it made her think, like that stern jaw and hard mouth sliding down her throat. "I like you just fine." Her voice was firm. "But sometimes you have to play by other people's rules to get things done."

"Right, of course." He looked like he wanted to say something else, but his clenched jaw kept any words from coming out.

She needed to change the subject to something he wasn't dead set against. They could work more on his behavior in public when he wasn't already on the defensive. "Are you free all afternoon?"

He relaxed and leaned forward, posture casual. "I've cleared my calendar just for you."

She didn't know if that was enticing or just arrogant. Or maybe both. She forced her demeanor to stay neutral. "Great. I was thinking we'd go shopping. Get you something more appropriate to wear to business meetings."

"You're going to show me how to dress." It wasn't a question.

She pursed her lips. "It's not like I'm going to

throw out your jeans, though if you've got any that are rattier than that, you probably can't wear them in public anyway. You just need a couple of Oxfords and some slacks for when it's appropriate." She kept the tailored suit suggestion to herself. One step at a time.

"Of course." He winked at her. "When do we play *My Fair Lady*?" His voice grew shrill. "The rain in Spain falls mainly on the plain." He enunciated every word, drawing another round of glares from nearby tables.

A musical reference. That held promise. But his delivery wasn't doing it for her. She lowered her voice, leaning over the table and growling. "Stop. You need to learn how to behave in public instead of acting like a spoiled frat boy with a trust fund."

"So sorry." His playful expression vanished, and his lips clamped shut.

He genuinely looked wounded. Why had she said that? And if he stopped listening, how was she going to get her point across?

An awkward silence descended over them. When the waitress brought out their appetizer, Scott was just as friendly and brash as before, and Kenzie wanted to plug her fingers in her ears and crawl under the table at the graphic conversation about breast feeding and pumping.

Tanya left, and Scott sighed. He dipped a battered piece of squid in sauce and chewed thoughtfully. He nodded at the bar. "See the bottles lining the back wall?"

Kenzie glanced at the multicolored glass for a brief second and then went back to staring at her plate. "Yes."

"Michele—the man who owns the bar—collects them. Every time he visits a new city or country, he makes it a point to find a gorgeous wine bottle, something unique, to add to his collection. He's got killer stories about every one of them."

Kenzie wanted to ask more, but fear of saying the wrong thing again kept her from diving into the conversation. She wanted to do playful banter and get her job done at the same time. Was that too much to ask? "They're very pretty."

Scott shrugged. "Are you going to have any calamari?"

She shook her head.

"You're not allergic are you? You should have said something."

"I'm not allergic."

He nodded toward a side window. It faced an alley lined with cars. Several plant boxes decorated the bottom of the plate glass, diluting the ugliness on the other side.

"Do you like the flowers?" he asked.

What was he doing? "They're flowers. They're pretty enough."

Her lack of input didn't seem to deter him. "The fuchsia ones only bloom for about a week, and always this time of year. They've always been one of my favorites. Bright and vibrant and not afraid to take a stand when it's time, fading back when it's someone else's turn."

She studied his face, looking for some sort of hint that he was trying to tell her something, but his blank expression stared back. Still, she was mildly impressed he knew what fuchsia was. She nodded toward a different box of flowers. "I like the violets better."

The corner of his mouth pulled up. "I'm not surprised."

Presumptuous ass. "Oh?"

He speared another piece of calamari and dipped it in sauce, but didn't eat it. "They match your purse. In fact, every time I've seen you, you've been wearing something that color, even if it was just the elastic you held back your ponytail with."

He had noticed? She couldn't deny the flutter in her chest. Maybe that was his problem then. He was so resistant to change because he was gay and couldn't admit it to himself or something. Memories of the day before taunted her—his strong hands sliding over her curves, the way he kissed her … she flushed. No, she was pretty sure he was straight.

He leaned across the table, holding out the fork. "Just take one bite?"

She accepted with the warmth inside growing as he fed her.

"Well?" He watched her hopefully.

She made a presentation of chewing and swallowing, washing it down with a sip of wine. "It's really good," she admitted begrudgingly. Like, really good. She wasn't used to her seafood being prepared so well. She grabbed her own fork and took another bite.

His foot brushed her shin under the table, and he winked at her. "Careful, your professionally crafted mask is slipping."

She overlooked the subtle jab in favor of

concentrating on the brief, teasing contact. "I did some research on you last night."

He twirled his straw in his drink, ice clinking against the glass. "Sounds like a boring read."

"Actually, it was really interesting. Two kids barely in their twenties find the funding to make it big in the software industry, only to have it ripped away by a spiteful ex-girlfriend and a vicious competitor. And then to come back and do it a second time before you were thirty. I'm impressed."

His focus stayed on his glass. "It was something I believed in, so I made it happen."

Was he actually embarrassed? She was starting to wonder if he was capable. "It is a big deal. It reads like a high-stakes fairytale. But one thing did make me curious."

He looked straight at her, dark eyes searching for something. "All that and only one thing stood out?"

He wasn't embarrassed, he was proud. And those eyes, she forced her gaze away. "Fair enough. A lot of things stood out. But you don't seem to publicly exist before your first company became a name. Like no yearbook photos, no college, no anything. Is there a reason your past is hidden?"

He shrugged. "It's not. My parents divorced a few years ago. It was messy and I'd never been fond of my father anyway, so I legally changed my last name to my mother's maiden name. My entire childhood is probably still out there."

That wasn't nearly as interesting as she'd expected. At least some of his surprises weren't bad. "So what's your old name?"

"Lunch," Tanya interrupted, setting a plate in front of her.

"Thanks." Scott flashed the waitress a smile.

Kenzie's shoulders slumped, and she sank back in her chair. Things were about to get loud again. There was no way he'd even listen if she tried to shush him now. Except he kept his voice low and the conversation brief. She hid her smile behind her glass as she took another sip of wine.

Waitress gone, he turned his full attention back to her. "So, clothes shopping, really?"

She laughed at his feigned disgust. "I promise to try and keep it from being boring."

"Not possible. Did you have a destination in mind?"

Finally, something she knew that he didn't. It was a small thing, but she'd take her victories where she could find them. "It's a surprise."

"Give me a hint?" His smile never wavered.

"It's not Hot Topic."

He raised an eyebrow. "Glad to hear it."

She pushed her half-finished wine aside and grabbed her ice water instead.

He brushed her shin with his foot again, lingering longer this time. "Not to turn the tables on you or anything, but I'm tired of talking about me. Tell me about yourself. I already know you're from here. Just the one sister?"

He didn't miss a lot, and it made her smile to know he'd remembered such small details from previous conversations. She took a small bite of the food, considering her answer. It was as good as the appetizer had been, and her stomach grumbled in appreciation. "Yes. No brothers."

"Older or younger?"

Did he really care? The sincerity in his eyes said yes. The revelation added to her lilting mood. "Older by five minutes."

"Twins." He raised an eyebrow. "Identical?"

"Physically."

"Right." His attention was completely on her, his lunch untouched. "So she's the one who usually picks up strangers, does the one-night-stand thing, the irresponsible stuff."

"I—" She paused, not sure if she was about to defend herself or Riley. "As you're so fond of pointing out, I approached you."

He stared back in disbelief, his familiar crooked smile in place. "And you've also confessed it was completely out of character for you."

"Does it matter if I'd ever done it before?"

"It does to me." He picked at his vegetables. "I like thinking I was your first for something. It's good for a guy's ego, right?"

How did he always manage to make conversation so easy? She laughed at the teasing. "Like your ego needs help."

"Sometimes it does." His eyes grew wide, his feigned hurt ruined by the twitch of his mouth. "I'm a delicate flower."

"Why are you always so direct?" She had asked him the question once before, but she wanted more of an answer.

His gaze raked over her face as if he was trying to peer into her thoughts. "Chicks dig honesty, right?"

"No," she corrected him. "Chicks only think they dig honesty until it includes something they don't want to hear."

"It worked on you."

Arrogant ass. The thought didn't have any malice in it. "You got lucky."

He snorted. "Damn straight. And I wouldn't mind getting lucky again."

She rolled her eyes and shook her head, but couldn't lose her smile. "Seriously, it has to be counterproductive most the time."

"I'll answer your question if you tell me something. Where do you usually meet guys?"

She stared back, confused about the gentle curve in the conversation. "Why?"

He pushed his barely touched plate aside. "Let's see … probably not business meetings, that would be inappropriate. And I can't see you spending much time in bars. We can add coffee shops to the list."

"You were the only one."

"I knew it."

She slapped his hand playfully. "Yes, fine. You were a first. Happy?"

"Immensely. Where did you meet your last boyfriend? The bookstore or something?"

Heat flooded her cheeks, and she ducked her head. It had been a lucky guess, that was all.

He laughed. "I was kidding. I'm right, seriously?"

"Yes, I met my last boyfriend at the bookstore."

"The relationship section?"

She twisted her mouth in irritation and just glared at him. "Fiction and literature."

"Bronte?" he asked.

"Vonnegut."

He raised an eyebrow. "So what was the first thing he said to you?"

Why were they having this conversation? Not that she minded, but she was still trying to figure out his random tangents. "I don't remember."

"You're lying." There was no accusation in the words, it was a simple statement.

She looked at him, eyes wide. How had he known that? "It was something about how Vonnegut had nothing on William Gibson when it came to the cynical but not completely fatalistic future of the planet. And I told him that wasn't a fair comparison because Kurt Vonnegut was absolutely a fatalistic literary genius and William Gibson was some sciency guy."

His jaw dropped. "You called the father of cyber punk a sciency guy? I mean, I guess technically you're right, but you said that?"

Finally she had caught him off-guard. "And his reaction was a lot like yours. Don't get me wrong, William Gibson is fantastic, but it's still like comparing Apples and Windows."

She wasn't sure why she'd tossed the reference in to mangle the cliché. It wasn't like she cared if he knew she had any sort of geek cred.

"Nice." His shock faded back into amusement. "And you went out with him after that."

"For a while." She didn't want to get into the details. She was over the guy, but there was no reason to divulge she'd dumped him because he was boring in bed.

"So, last guy you didn't go out with—the most recent one you've turned down. What was the first thing he said to you?"

"Like I remember. Maybe, *do those legs go all the way up*?" The background noise had faded as the lunchtime crowd thinned, and she was grateful she didn't have anywhere else to be.

"But you let the guy who asked you about your honeyed walls give you a lift home."

And she realized what he was doing—trying to point out to her why it was wrong to try and change him for the sake of appearance. He seemed fond of the object lesson rather than the direct answer. "Yes. Because you were sincere, and the guy in the bookstore was sincere—both of you inflammatory—but still sincere, and those assholes with the lines were just saying what they thought I wanted to hear."

"I've made my point?" He didn't look smug.

"Yes." She took another drink. "But I'm still going to teach you to behave in public. You're not learning to pick up women. You're learning to keep your investors happy."

He leaned in, voice low. "I already know the legs go all the way because how awkward would that be if they didn't?" An underlying current ran through his words. "But if I told you that you had a beautiful body, would you forget this mission of yours?"

"You mean my job?" The way he'd twisted the otherwise horrid line added to her enjoyment, and the underlying compliment warmed her more than the wine had. "No. But don't let that stop you from trying."

"You've really read William Gibson." He

switched gears without pause.

"I prefer Philip K. Dick, but *Neuromancer* has a special place on my bookshelf. I was in a really weird frame of mind the first time I read it, it kind of screwed with my head, and I haven't been able to forget it since."

The rough canvas of a High Top traced up the back of her calf, sending a pleasant chill through her. His expression softened, eyes pulling up at the corners. "I know the feeling."

chapter seven

A folded blanket stared back at Scott in his rearview mirror. It would probably be there for a while—he like the memories associated with it. He glanced at Kenzie out of the corner of his eye. Had she noticed? Only the obvious really seemed to escape her, so probably not.

He'd frozen inside when she'd brought up his past and was glad she'd let him change the subject so quickly. It wasn't like he'd come from a battered home, not in the traditional sense. He'd had it all growing up—money, the best education available, and almost two decades of the finest food, clothes, and friends money could buy.

He glanced at Kenzie as the unpleasant memories tripped through his thoughts. The corners of her mouth were pulled up in an almost smile. She wouldn't tell him where they were going, only that Hot Topic wasn't an appropriate place for someone like him to shop. He wasn't sure what made *him* different from anyone who worked for him, but he hadn't bothered to tell her the only thing he owned from Hot Topic was a pair of panda mittens someone had given him as a gag gift a few years ago. Maybe he'd dig those up tomorrow just for kicks.

But that was the thing about his childhood. His father was first-generation money—having started as a mechanic to support his mother when he'd gotten her pregnant right before high school graduation. But Dad was bright and had managed to spin the opportunity quickly, growing his name and reputation into the face of one of the largest car dealership chains in the western states.

He'd wanted Scott to have everything he hadn't. Including connections, the knowledge to be able to perform on demand, and the ability to mold himself to what the "right" people expected of him.

And Scott might not have resented it if that upbringing hadn't included countless hours of being told playing video games would never get him anywhere in life, and that the only way to be someone important was to wear the mask the people with the money expected to see.

"Park here." Kenzie's request jarred him back to the present. She was pointing to a row of spots in front of Nordstrom.

"Yes ma'am." He did as he was told, keeping a teasing lilt to his response.

He followed her into the store, past racks of designer labels and women who reminded him of his mother—straight posture, well-coifed silver hair, and gold and diamonds sparkling from their wrists and fingers—to the men's department.

Plastic torsos in button-down shirts and silk ties stared down at them from high shelves on the walls. Scott would have told her this wasn't where he really wanted to be, but she would have misunderstood.

Assumed he was being difficult and not just picky.

Displays dotted the area, but no actual racks, and a counter sat in the middle of it all, a familiar young man scanning the shop, doing a decent job of hiding his boredom.

A smile lit his hazel eyes when Scott and Kenzie approached, and he stepped away from his watch post. "Mr. McAllister, I didn't realize you'd be in today. What can I do for you?"

Scott returned the smile. "Hey, Evan. I didn't either." Scott nodded at Kenzie. "This young lady isn't as fond of my T-shirt as I am. Grab whatever she asks for?"

"Is there anywhere in this valley you aren't on a first name basis with the staff?" Kenzie's voice was a low rasp, only meant for his ears.

He glanced at her, relieved that her cheeks were still flushed with amusement. "There's a Village Inn on State and one-oh-sixth that I don't think I've been in since I was a teenager."

Her lips twitched as she struggled to hold back a smile, and her gaze travelled over him.

His blood pressure increased, and he shoved his hands into his pockets to give himself something else to focus on. Between that appraising glance and her full lips, he was wishing they were anywhere but a public place.

"You're what, a 34/34?" she asked.

She was good. He bit back the offer to let her measure his inseam herself if she wanted to find out. "That's right."

She turned back to Evan. "We need some slacks, a couple of Izods and Oxfords, though oddly enough I think we're okay on the sport jacket front."

Evan blinked, friendly smile frozen in place. "For him?"

Scott swallowed his laugh at the disbelief. Evan was forever giving him a hard time about being too good to buy his clothes off the rack like a pleeb. Childhood had left some impressions he couldn't shake—like formal and business attire should be tailored. Fortunately, since he'd rather spend his money on other things, he didn't have to make those purchases often. "For me."

Evan gave him one last glance and then shook his head. "Of course. I'll be right back."

"What was that about?" Kenzie asked as soon as Evan was gone.

Scott shrugged. "Maybe I should have mentioned we've got a corporate account. We send our people here when they need to look good for trade shows, meetings, whatever. I'm just not usually one of them."

Kenzie shook her head, and her expression was a bizarre combination of disbelief and what he would have called fascination on anyone else. Maybe he should tell her that was almost—but not quite—as attractive as the lip biting, or the blushing. With every shift in her expression, his pulse raced a little faster, drawing his attention from the task at hand and tempting him with what they could get up to if they took another afternoon off.

She stepped away, wandering around the department, occasionally paying attention to a display tie, or running a finger down a headless torso—he assumed checking the fabric of the shirt.

What he wouldn't give to be that mannequin right then, lower body or not. At least the plastic dummy didn't have to worry about how impossible it currently was to sate the pulse below his waist, or deal with the lightheadedness that came from all his blood rushing to his cock.

Scott tried to be discreet about adjusting his jeans. They needed to buy this stuff and get out of here.

Kenzie glanced back at him and nodded at the shirt/tie combination next to her, elongating the stretch of her neck. "What about this?" Her cheeks and lips were flushed with the genuine fun she seemed to be having.

What he actually thought was that the two blues were different hues and clashed. But the creeping lust disagreed, thinking whatever she wanted him to if he could run his mouth over the hollow at the base of her throat. "I trust your judgment."

"I have a dressing room set up." Evan returned, interrupting the moment. "This way."

Of course she was going to want him to try the stuff on. Now he was going to have to play dress-up doll. What would she do if he told her the slacks might not fit quite right just now? "Can't you just tell him sizes and colors, and we can buy them and leave?" He followed them toward a room in back.

"No." Kenzie gave him a look that said there was no way she'd consider that. "We have to know how they hang, fit, work together."

"We have a couple of ties that aren't out yet that would look great with those shirts," Evan said. "I'll go grab them if you're interested."

"You've got a good eye for these things." Scott kept his voice low enough for only Kenzie to hear. "I'm sure they all look great together."

She didn't yield. "Please do." Kenzie smiled at Evan.

And Evan was gone again.

"The faster you get this over with, the faster you can be rid of me for the day." Kenzie nudged him into the dressing room.

A shock of want raced through him when her hand brushed his arm, and he tried to ignore it. On second thought, what were the odds he could make the afternoon serve two purposes?

"They look great. There, we're done." His refusal to cooperate lacked conviction.

Her lips drew into a thin line. "It won't kill you to try them on."

Inspiration was pulsing through him. He grabbed her wrists loosely, inhaling sharply at the heat of her skin against his palms, and tugged her into the dressing room. He kicked the door shut. "I think I need help."

He kept his grip casual enough to let her pull away, and desire throbbed under his skin when she smiled instead of trying to leave.

She grabbed the bottom of his shirt, palms brushing his bare waist, her voice low. "The whole concept of buttons has you confused?"

He hissed at the teasing contact, and dipped his head next to hers, lips hovering near her ear while he whispered, "You're sweet to play along, but you know what I think we should do instead?"

She shook her head. "You mean you don't

really need help trying on clothes?"

"Probably not. Instead, I think we should pretend we're those two people from the coffee shop last weekend. The two who are practicing not being frigid."

She licked her lips, but didn't close the distance between them. "That sounds distinctly counterproductive and unprofessional."

"So why are you still here?" He took a step back. "I can probably figure out the buttons myself."

"Probably?" She closed the distance between them.

"Maybe." His pulse was screaming in anticipation. He trailed his fingers down her spine, coming to a rest in the small of her back and holding her close. "Maybe not."

Her "I think I should supervise" was breathy.

He tangled his fingers in her hair and tugged, her gasp spurring him on. His mouth slid down her throat, her pulse racing and throbbing against his lips.

Someone knocked on the dressing room door. "I have those ties," Evan said.

"Great." Scott's reply came out gruffer than he expected. "Leave them out there, and we'll let you know if we need anything else."

♥♥♥

Kenzie was more irritated than she expected with the interruption. The hungry growl in Scott's reply sent desire screaming through her. She shouldn't be doing this, it was so very wrong. But his strong hands and the way he'd controlled the situation from the moment they'd walked into the store had every inch of her begging for more.

"Now that he's gone…" He turned his full attention back to her, tugging her hair and kissing her hungrily. She bit back a whimper and ground against him. His arousal dug into her hip, making the warmth between her legs spread.

His hands slid down her sides, past the edge of her skirt, and he pushed the hem up, fabric biting into her skin and burning with friction as it rose over her hips. He let out a short laugh and grazed her neck with his teeth. "Knowing that you're wearing these thigh-highs makes it so hard to behave myself."

She leaned her head back, gasping as he sucked on the skin between her neck and shoulder. "You say that like it's a bad thing."

"Not even close." He lifted her leg and hooked it around his hip, stepping back close enough to the bench to let her rest her foot on it. His hand glided up the back of her thigh, his skin rough against hers. His fingers brushed the edge of her butt and slid forward.

"You know." His whisper caressed the outside of her ear, his voice low and full of want. "I still fantasize about your moans that morning on the beach. What are the odds I can make you that loud again?"

The power and aggression in his question heightened her arousal. "Not likely. Not here." Her voice was barely audible even to her own ears. The thrill of being someplace public raced through her, but she wasn't interested even for a moment in getting caught.

His chuckle rumbled through the base of her throat as he slid his lips up her collarbone. "That sounds like a challenge."

His hand crept around her thigh, brushing the outside of the already damp white cotton that was the only thing keeping him from Kenzie's ache. She knew what he could do with those fingers.

He dropped back onto the padded bench behind him. He rested one hand against her butt and pulled her closer. With her foot on the bench he was eye level with her waist. He brushed her skin when he traced a finger along the crotch of her panties and then shoved the fabric aside. His tongue trailed along the same path, and she arched her back at the sensation.

He found her aching button and flicked back and forth across it. She had to bite her lip to keep from moaning out loud. A wave of disappointment crashed over her when he stopped, but it didn't last long as he plunged inside her, licking her inner walls. His thumb found its way to her clit instead, massaging hard.

Climax built inside her rapidly, rushing through her without warning. Her fingers tangled in his hair, holding his face close as she thrust against him, legs suddenly growing weak as she peaked.

She pulled away from his touch slowly, shuddering with each brush of his thumb against the now hyper-sensitive region. A tiny exhale escaped, but still she kept her voice down.

She was grateful when he ran a hand down the back of her shaky leg and lowered it to the ground. He grabbed a cellophane square from his wallet and rested his hands on her hips, pulling her down so she was straddling his legs and hovering over his lap.

"Do you have any idea how desperately I want to be inside you right now?" he growled in her ear. "To feel you wrapped around me?"

She didn't have a clever comeback, so she pressed her mouth to his, tasting the lingering traces of herself as she kissed him hard enough her teeth scraped the inside of her lips. She reached between their legs to slide down his zipper. He groaned against her mouth when her fingers found his rigid shaft, working it loose from its prison. His hand joined hers, brushing between her legs again as he slid on the condom.

His head hovered right at the edge of her eager opening, and she let out a sharp gasp when he plunged deep inside, stretching her out and filling her up.

She rocked slowly against him. His fingers traced up her chest, undoing the top two buttons on her blouse. He sucked and kissed along the exposed skin. Every time he thrust inside her, he hit something deep. His hips ground with increased pace and need, and she rode him to match the intensity. She felt another wave rush through her, this one slower, and clenched her jaw to keep her moans from escaping.

He slammed inside her, mouth pressed into her chest, her skin absorbing and vibrating from his grunts. She clenched around him as she climaxed a second time, still pushing hard, wanting to ride the feeling out.

He jerked hard and fast until his rhythm slowed and then came to a stop.

He rested his cheek against her ribs, breathing

heavy. She laid her head on top of his, not able to think of anything to say. That had been such a bad idea. So why didn't she regret it?

He slipped out of her as he softened, and after a few minutes, she found the strength in her legs to stand. She struggled to keep her voice even as she straightened her clothes and hair in the full-length mirror behind him. "I should let you try this stuff on."

He leaned back, head resting against the mirror, and studied her with an unreadable expression on his face. "Yes, ma'am."

She stepped out of the dressing room and latched the door shut behind her. The department was empty—even Evan had vanished—so why did she feel like everyone in the world knew what they had just done? Even worse, why didn't she care? Instead, she felt a whisper of guilt at the defeat in the voice of the man she'd left in the other room. Guilt and the overwhelming desire to find the next place they could get away with that. Preferably somewhere she wouldn't have to be quiet.

chapter eight

Scott tugged on the sleeves of the tailored jacket and stretched his neck. It wasn't that it didn't fit well, it just didn't fit as well as some of those he had in his closet. Still, Kenzie had picked it out, and he was putting on the playing-nice face, so he might as well wear it at least once.

Besides, they were meeting with Hank Cartee, and Scott wanted to reinforce the fact that he was obeying the board's edict.

Zach joined him on the sidewalk outside the restaurant, looking him up and down with a raised eyebrow. "What did you do, buy a suit at Nordstrom?"

They always met about ten minutes before business dinners to make sure they were both on the same page. Scott shrugged. "I'm just doing what my keeper tells me."

Zach shook his head. "Right. A department store suit is the way to do this right?"

Scott smirked. His best friend had the same appreciation for the European suits that Scott did, but sometimes Zach was too much of a snob about the whole thing. Scott ran his thumbs under the lapels of the double-breasted jacket. "Kenzie picked it. She's proud of herself."

Zach didn't look convinced, but he didn't say anything else. Instead, he nodded toward the parking lot. "Speaking of."

She was strolling toward them in heels that put her at eye level with Scott. Her black dress hugged her curves and flared out at the hips, ending just below the knees. A shrug topped her outfit off, ending below her breasts and making the outfit look professional but alluring. He hoped she was wearing stockings like the other day. The memory was enough to add a layer of ambivalence to his dread about the night ahead. Something inside still ached when he remembered how she'd pulled away abruptly after they'd finished in the dressing room.

Zach let out a soft whistle. "Damn."

Scott elbowed him. "Keep it down." But he couldn't take his eyes off her. Her hair was pulled back, with just a few strands left loose in soft ringlets to frame her face. Her blue eyes locked on his as she drew within earshot, and she flashed him a quick smile before ducking her head and turning away.

"What's she doing here?" Scott's question was barely a whisper.

Zach smirked at him. "She's our insurance policy. Proof that we're doing what Cartee wanted."

"Gentlemen." Kenzie extended her hand, greeting Zach first and then Scott. She kept her distance from both, and her voice was cool and calm.

"Ah, the men of the hour." A booming voice bounced off asphalt.

Scott hid his wince and pasted a grin in place as

Hank Cartee approached. The other man was several inches shorter, but just as broad-chested as Scott, and carried himself like he was the only person in a room. His blond hair was thinning on top, but he'd grown it long enough to comb it over, insisting it was surfer trendy. Scott didn't even know what that meant.

"And who is this stunning young lady?" Hank's gaze raked over Kenzie, lingering several seconds on her chest and never quite making it to her face.

"Mackenzie Carter, publicity." She shook his hand. Her smile had cooled several degrees, Scott noted with a hint of satisfaction.

The four continued to chat as they made their way inside and were seated. Or rather, three of them chatted and Scott watched, reminded more with every passing second why he wasn't fond of Hank.

"So you're shaping that dipshit into something presentable, are you?" Hank had taken the chair next to Kenzie and angled it toward her. His arms rested on the edge of the table, gaze locked just below her neck.

Hypocritical asshole. For a moment—as he frequently did during these meetings—Scott wished he still drank. He focused on his water and hoped he could be polite when appropriate.

"No." Kenzie turned away from him, watching the table even though she was still answering his question. "But Mr. McAllister has been great to work with. It's almost like he knows all of this already, and he's just tolerating me."

Scott nearly choked on his drink as his eyes met hers across the table. There was no way she'd figured that out. The flat expression on her face told him no, she hadn't. She was just playing the part.

"Maybe when you're done with him, we could have you do more for the rest of the company. I'm sure you've got a couple of things you could teach me." Hank brushed his hand over hers, reaching for the bread basket.

Scott couldn't do this. Ten minutes into dinner and he already wanted to punch the asshole in the face. He pushed back quietly, not wanting to draw too much attention. "If you'll excuse me, I have a call to make before things get too hectic overseas."

Kenzie's eyes grew wide for a moment before her icy mask slipped back into place. Zach gave him a warning look.

Hank waved a dismissive hand. "You do what you have to."

Scott gritted his teeth as he headed toward a spot near the back of the restaurant he knew would be quiet. Behind him, he heard a few more snatches of conversation and had to bite back a retch.

Kenzie's voice was cold, but polite. "I'll give you my company's name. They can put you in touch with someone more familiar with group work."

"I'd rather see what you can do one-on-one first." Hank sounded like a snake that had learned to enunciate.

Kenzie had worked with leeches before. Self-proclaimed gentlemen who assumed if she was there to whip their image into shape, she was there for all their needs. She'd never had an issue telling them where to stick it instead and walking away. But that had always been her contract to break, not a multi-million dollar investment deal for someone else. And to top it all off, this was the jerk who had accused Scott of not knowing how to behave in public.

When Hank's hand found her knee under the table and then slid higher, she couldn't sit still anymore. She tried to be polite about pulling away. "I'm so sorry. I need to powder my nose."

Zach stood when she did.

Hank nodded up at her and turned his attention to his drink. "Hurry back. We've got business to discuss."

Heat flooded her entire body, fury pumping through every inch. She ducked into the restroom, relieved it was empty, and splashed cold water on her face. Her reflection blinked back at her, drops streaming down smeared cheeks, flushed red glaring through it all. She wiped away the destroyed makeup and set out to reapply as quickly as she could, hoping the familiar motions would numb her thoughts.

Or maybe she shouldn't bother with the touch-up. She couldn't believe she was even considering bailing for the night, but she wasn't helping by being there. She'd made the point; she'd proven Scott was trying. Her presence was just distracting from the boys talking.

Had she really just thought that? She wanted to slap herself. She could play with the big boys as well as anyone else, and some bozo like Hank Cartee wasn't going to intimidate her. She wasn't some executive's dainty wife who was only there to look pretty. Taking a deep breath, she finished touching up her makeup and braced herself for the rest of the evening. She could find a way to put him in his place without costing anyone anything. It was what she did.

As she emerged from the bathroom, a flash of gray fabric caught her attention on the edge of her peripheral vision. She spun and saw Scott loitering in a corner, back against the wall, raking his fingers through his hair. She was still happy he'd worn the suit she picked out. It accentuated his broad shoulders and made him look distinguished instead of intimidating. Not that intimidating was always bad in his case.

She pushed the thought away. She needed to focus on the night, not on him. She also needed to drag him back to dinner.

He jumped a little, eyes wide when she stopped in front of him. "Hey." His smile was weak, but his voice was warm.

"I think your associates are looking for you." She nodded toward the dining room. He'd picked an out-of-sight place to hide, and there was less than a foot between them. He radiated a subtle hint of cologne and a more powerful impression of panic. This was why she was here. To get him through the night. She just had to remember that.

"I think it's more likely they're looking for you." Scott's laugh was forced. "Zach has a pretty good idea where I am. And I'm really sorry about Cartee. I mean, he's right that you look incredible, but that's no excuse for him to let so much of himself show."

She ducked her head at the compliment. Why did it sound so much more genuine, and less repulsive, coming from him? Maybe it was because his eyes never left hers.

His finger rested under her chin, and he pulled her face back up. His tone was kind. "I wouldn't blame you if you made some excuse and hightailed it out of here. I'll go with you if it will help."

It was more tempting than she dared dwell on. "I thought about it, believe me." She let out a short laugh. "But if you can tolerate the rest of the evening, so can I." Except she didn't want to head back out there. She wanted him to push her against the wall and kiss her, and make her have to bite back screams, and … she forced the thoughts away.

His thumb traced under her eye, and his voice dropped in volume. "Your makeup's smudged. Are you sure you're all right?"

She covered his hand with hers, meaning to push him away, but lingering instead. "I'm fine, I promise." Her pulse hammered in her ears, making it difficult to hear anything but him.

He pulled away, palm brushing her shoulder and sending a tremor through her as he dropped his arm. "We should probably get back."

But he didn't move.

"Probably." Neither did she. There was something hidden in his brown eyes she wanted to dive into and discover. What was it?

"There you two are." Hank's brash announcement startled her. "Making out in a dark corner, really?"

Kenzie's fury returned full force. Apparently she didn't have it as under control as she thought. She backed away. "I should get back." But Hank had blocked them in.

"I knew you were high school, McAllister, but even a virgin newb knows you don't get to kiss the escort on the lips." Hank's insult carried, echoing off plaster. "I should have known you weren't taking this seriously, but paying someone to pretend so you don't have to actually follow through, and you can't even wait for your happy ending until you get home?"

Kenzie's hands clenched into fists, and a string of exactly what she thought of this snake rushed to the tip of her tongue. But the vulgarities never got a chance to spill out.

Scott grabbed Hank's jacket near the shoulder and swung him into the wall with a quiet *thunk*. "I assure you, I'm taking this very seriously." Scott's voice was a low growl, barely audible above the clatter of silverware against plates from the nearest table, but the threat was unmistakable.

Hank's eyes were wide. "Let go. This suit is worth more than your car."

Scott snorted. "I really doubt that. But it doesn't matter how much money you have." Every word was spoken through gritted teeth, none meant for any ears but theirs. "It doesn't give you a right to talk to anyone like that, especially my people." His grip tightened, knuckles growing pale when Hank struggled to break away. "Just because you find your women on the corner of Ventura doesn't mean everyone does, and if you ever call anyone who works for me a whore again, the threat of assault charges that are keeping me from breaking your nose won't be a deterrent."

Hank's upper lip pulled into a sneer. "I'm surprised it's stopping you now. Control isn't your strong suit."

Scott let go, hand clenching into a fist and drawing back for a hook. Hank backed away quickly, almost tripping over his feet.

"The night is over, McAllister. I'll be talking to the board tomorrow." Cartee's back was straight, shoulders back as he headed for the exit, but he moved like the hounds of hell were on his heels.

"Thank you." Kenzie's voice was quiet, her hammering heart making it difficult to speak.

Scott just shook his head and pushed away. As she followed him to the table, she couldn't help but notice no one was watching them. Conversations were happening as if a fist fight hadn't almost broken out just a few feet from their seats. All that, and he'd still managed to keep it quiet. That man was such an enigma.

Zach half rose as they approached. "Did I miss something?"

Scott inhaled sharply. "Yes. I'm bailing. Call me."

"Wait." Kenzie reached for him but dropped her hand at his troubled expression. The conflicted hurt, confusion, anger, and frustration must have mirrored her own, and she didn't know if she was ready to face her own ambivalence, let alone his.

He followed the same path as Hank, disappearing outside in a matter of seconds.

Kenzie sank into her chair as everything caught up with her and her legs gave out.

Zach pointed at a plate of stuffed mushrooms.

"Help yourself."

How could he be so calm? Oh, right, because he didn't know what had happened. She knocked back her white wine, finishing the entire glass in a single swallow.

That made him raise an eyebrow. "What did I miss?"

Gawd, how was she supposed to explain what had happened? The words spilled out, jumbled and abrupt. "He called me a whore, and Scott threatened to deck him, and he said he was assembling the board."

Zach's lips drew into a thin line, and he sighed. "I'm sorry."

He looked as torn as she felt. "No, I am. You shouldn't have invited me tonight. I've cost you what you hired me to save. And I don't even, I just—"

"Stop." He cut her off, tone kind. "No you didn't, and it's not your fault. Never apologize because someone else can't control themselves."

She felt some of the stress drain from her shoulders as the wine worked its way through her. "But…"

He stabbed a mushroom and chewed thoughtfully, swallowing before he replied. "The two of them have never gotten along. It's times like this I wish we'd known that before we took Hank's money."

Kenzie frowned, but didn't argue. She knew how things worked in business.

"We've got a developer he likes." Zach leaned back, hands clasped and resting on the edge of the table. "The kid's a savant, and Cartee is forever trying to hire him away. We'll send him to California to play nice, they'll probably drop way more of our money than they should in tittie bars, and things will be back to a level three hostile instead of level one by next week."

Frustration and tears threatened, and she bit them back as exhaustion trickled in. Sometimes she really hated playing in what men saw as their world. "I see."

Zach's expression softened. "I really am genuinely sorry, and I wouldn't blame you if you dropped us. Hank's an ass, but I didn't expect this. Still, you're doing good things for Scott, I can tell, so I'll ask you to stay and leave the rest up to you."

He meant quit. She hadn't even considered it. But it sounded more tempting than it should. She needed to get away from this environment. It was screwing with her head in ways she'd never dealt with before. Not being able to keep her hands off a client? She knew better than that. She'd never even been tempted before. So why did the thought of walking away make her a little ill? Or maybe that was just the ebbing adrenaline settling in her gut.

She gave him a tired smile. "I honestly don't know. Give me the weekend to think about it?"

The corner of Zach's mouth pulled down, but he nodded. "Of course."

chapter nine

Kenzie's front door pushed back when she tried to open it, and she had to lean into it to get inside. She sighed at the sight of her sister's suitcases filling half the living room.

"Riley." Her tired voice carried through the apartment. She didn't need this tonight. Her brain was already fractured after dinner.

Her twin stuck her head out from the bathroom, a streak of bright pink running through her pale hair. "Hey. I thought you'd be out a lot longer."

"Why does my living room look like a refugee camp?" Kenzie didn't want to deal with this right now. Riley went through roommates and boyfriends—frequently the same thing in her case—like most people went through a large canister of sprouted wheat cereal. With hardcore enthusiasm at first, and then tossing it out after six months only half finished. Still, she had sworn there was something special this time and insisted that as soon as they made up, she'd be back in his arms and apartment again.

"Hang on." Riley ducked back into the bathroom.

Kenzie pushed aside a duffel bag and sank onto the couch while she listened to the shower run.

About ten minutes later, Riley was perched on the edge of the chair next to her, not bothering to move the box occupying the rest of it. "What's up?"

Kenzie nodded around the room. "Why is all of your crap violating my living room? I thought you were making up with Archer."

Riley shrugged and twirled a strand of damp, violently pink hair around her finger. She still hadn't specifically said what had happened between them. "It's just a rough patch. Once he misses me enough, we'll be fine again."

Kenzie wanted to scold her for the color in her hair—Riley's boss was going to hate that—or for the mess, or something, but she couldn't find it in her. She had decisions to make, a future to consider, a lot of pondering about whether or not she was ever going to see Scott again. For work, of course. She stood, and bags toppled back in to fill her now vacant spot. "Whatever. Just, if you can, stack as much of it into the corner as will fit, please? I need to be able to move in here."

Riley studied her for a moment, concern heavy in her blue eyes. "Are you all right?"

Kenzie shook her head. She wasn't in the mood to be lectured about being frigid again. As far as she knew, her sister would have left with the knight in shining armor instead of sulking away in defeat. "But I'll get over it." She trudged into her bedroom, locked the door behind her, and collapsed on her bed. When had all of this become so tiring?

She was jarred awake by a pounding. She

turned her head to the side until her eyes focused on the digital clock by her bed. She'd slept until nine? Her brain throbbed through her eyes, and her entire body felt like lead. Why was it still dark outside? Oh, right, she'd slept for about fifteen minutes. No wonder she felt like crap.

"You all right?" Heavy concern laced Riley's question.

Kenzie pushed out of bed, wincing as the combs that had held her hair back dug into her scalp. She yanked them out, unlocked the door, and collapsed back onto her mattress with a loud sigh. "Yeah, I'm good."

Riley took a seat next to her. "Are you sure? You seem high strung lately. Like even more than normal."

"I don't need this right now." Kenzie flopped onto her back and stared at the ceiling. "What do you want?"

"You're home early and you're all dressed up. Comb your hair out and let's go to the bar."

She realized Riley was wearing a denim skirt that barely covered her ass and a hot pink tank top that matched the new streak in her hair. "I don't think we're dressed to go to the same kind of bar. Besides, I thought you were trying to make things better with Archer."

"Better with Archer. Right." Riley stood and grabbed her hand, tugging her to her feet. "We're not going for me, we're going for you. You look sexy tonight, sis. I'll be your frumpy wingman. Wingwoman. Whatever. It'll be fun."

Kenzie smiled; it did sound like fun. She could

meet a guy, ignore his horrid pickup lines, and actually live a little instead of trying and failing. Or at the very least she could hang with her sister and unwind, and if any asshole implied she was a whore, she'd be within her rights to grind her stiletto into his toe and walk away. "All right, I'm in."

Kenzie propped her elbow on the bar and rested her chin in the palm of her hand. She tried to focus on the bottles lining the back wall instead of on Riley, who sat about six seats away, joking and laughing with a man who had bought her at least four drinks in the last hour.

Kenzie didn't look up when someone took the stool next to her.

"You know," his voice was warm and deep, with a hint of arrogance, "I don't normally like women who are taller than me, but the way you wear those heels is just so sexy."

She hid her wince and turned to face him. This was why she was here after all. He was certainly attractive—close-cut blond hair, pressed shirt, silk tie, and clear green eyes. She gave him a soft smile. "Thank you."

"What's your drink of choice tonight?" He nodded at her glass.

"Lime and tonic. I'm the designated driver."

He winked at her. "You can drive me."

Scott would have pulled that line off so much better. She hated herself for even thinking it. She needed to give this a chance, right? She was breaking away from the frigid and uptight her. It wouldn't hurt anyone to have some simple fun with this guy. "You're horrible." She giggled and held out her hand. "I'm Kenzie, by the way."

"Rod." His grip was strong, almost uncomfortably so, and his palm was cold. "You don't look like you're enjoying yourself."

It was her choice to accept or reject, she wasn't the aggressor anymore. She could do this. "I'm doing better now."

He ordered her another drink and himself a rum and Coke, paying for both. "So, Kenzie." His gaze raked over her. "Gorgeous woman like you buying her own drinks? What gives?"

Her skin felt like it was going to crawl off at the leer. He reminded her too much of Cartee. Where was Scott when she needed him? She banished the thought as soon as it surfaced. "My sister." She nodded over her shoulder. "Said I needed to unwind." Damn it, she shouldn't have said that. She knew what was coming even before he said anything. But maybe she'd be wrong. Please let her be wrong. She didn't want to be disappointed even further.

He looked in the direction she was nodding. "Twins, huh? That's hot."

She resisted the urge to slap her forehead. Nope, he'd said it. Why the hell did guys think sisters making out was sexy? "Not so much." She slid off her stool. "I need to be somewhere else."

"Wait." His cold palm against her arm made her skin recoil. "I'm sorry. I'm nervous, you know? Beautiful woman, so I'm trying to play it cool."

"Yeah, probably a mistake." She sat anyway. "How about you being you? I like guys who are themselves." Like Scott. The name echoed in her skull, and she pushed it away. Scott was a child playing the part she told him to. And not even willingly or well. Except for that suit he'd worn to dinner… No that was a bad path to go down. That was business, this was fun.

"I can do honesty. How about this? I'm really not into the random strangers or doing the one-night-stand thing, so I'm trying to pretend I'll be okay if you don't call me in the morning, but I'd really like to get to know you better."

He wanted something long-term, how sweet. She kept her smile pasted in place. Maybe if she pretended to enjoy the conversation, she'd start to believe it was true. He was attractive. He'd hold up to professional scrutiny; she could do the same for him. And then she'd have an excuse to turn Scott down. Not that she needed an excuse. It wasn't like she couldn't control herself around him.

She realized he was watching her. Crap, had he said something? He must have, he was waiting for a response. "Beg your pardon?"

He pushed his drink away and stepped from his stool, offering his arm. "It's a little loud here. Do you want to go somewhere else so we can talk?"

"That sounds nice." She slipped her hand into his arm, searching for the familiar rush of meeting someone new. It wasn't there. She was probably still too wired from dinner. She fell into step beside him as he led her outside. The night air and silence rushed in around them, and for a moment she thought she'd gone deaf.

She hesitated.

He looked at her, curious. "Are you all right?"

"No, I'm sorry." She dropped her hand, letting it hang limply by her side. "I…" She trailed off. What was wrong with her? "I can't after all. Have a wonderful night."

She turned toward the parking lot without waiting for a response. She pulled out her phone while she walked and sent her sister a quick message. She didn't want to ruin Riley's night too. *I have to bail, I'm sorry. Call a cab. I'll pay you back for it.*

chapter ten

Morning sun warmed Scott's back as it crested the mountains outside. It crept through the bay window behind him, permeating the shades meant to keep light out but still let people see through the large windows. He stared at the donut in front of him as people chattered in the crowded coffee shop. The wooden chair was one of the few in the eclectic dining area with no padding, but he barely noticed the hard seat against his back.

Every time he thought back to the night before, his blood pressure spiked. He didn't know if he was more upset with Hank, or with Zach for having the balls to ask Kenzie to stay on. No, he did know. He still wanted to hop the next plane to LA to grind Cartee into a bloody pulp. But this whole publicity facade was a freaking joke. He didn't even know why he was pretending anymore.

He pushed his donut and coffee aside and pulled out his PSP. He should be game testing. Right. Getting some work done would take his mind off things. He waited for the load screen and clicked into his latest save file. He needed to know if the physics were working on this level, whether or not the game play was too complicated this early on, if the means to defeat the end-level boss were clear without being too obvious…

If he should call Kenzie and apologize, if he should find a way to kick Cartee off the board…

A sniper's bullet tore through his character, and his screen splattered red. He snarled at the device and set it aside with a sigh. That was only about the twentieth time that had happened in the last half hour. Probably not a good sign.

The jangle of the front door mingled with the chatter around him, and he looked up. His mood twisted into something he couldn't identify when he saw Kenzie make her way to the counter. Like so many mornings, her hair was in a ponytail, and her sweatshirt was tied around her waist, showing off a white tank top that hugged her perfectly.

And she was staring intently at the menu, jaw set, face tight. No one should look that tense on a Saturday morning. Maybe if the two of them found someplace quiet she'd let him tear that hair elastic out…

He pushed the thought away. It was probably time for him to find a new one-night stand. One that actually only lasted one night.

Or an actual girlfriend, he hadn't had one of those in a while. Then he could prove he was all mature and shit like was expected of him. That ought to make Kenzie happy. Someone to use him as a dress-up doll twenty-four seven and keep him in line when she wasn't around. Oh, right, he always got tired of those women ages before they became long-term relationships.

She placed her order and turned, and his hand shot up in a wave before he could talk himself out of it. She hesitated, catching her bottom lip between her teeth, and then wove her way over. She took the seat across from him, sitting up so straight her back never touched the chair.

"Morning." Her expression was flat.

"Hey." He hated the lack of anything coming from her, but it was appropriate he supposed. "I'm sorry again about last night."

"You and everyone but the one guy who should be." She pursed her lips. "But thank you for stepping in. I wish it hadn't come to that."

A question tried to force itself past his lips, and he bit it back. He wasn't going to ask whether or not she'd decided to stay on. There was no reason to pressure her. Or to even care. If she decided no, he could go back to doing what he wanted when and how he wanted.

"How's the game coming along?" She nodded at his handheld.

"It's good. Hopefully a hit, but it's hard to tell before the sales numbers start coming in." Disappointment wormed through him, and it took him a moment to realize it was because she hadn't scolded him yet for the ratty camo pants, or stained white T-shirt, or for playing his game without ear buds, or anything. And she had yet to smile. "So, um, how have you been?"

Her mouth twisted in dry amusement. "It's been twelve hours. Not a lot has changed."

A shift in mood, a chink in her shell. He leaped at the chance to widen it. "You're sure. You haven't changed jobs, gotten engaged, started a family?"

Her smile threatened to become full-formed. "No. Though there was this guy…"

After less than twelve hours? Why did that send a dull thud through his chest? He kept the reaction from his face, but he couldn't hold back the subtle dig. "Sounds enticing. I bet he was a spiffy, well-dressed gentleman."

She gave a small laugh. "Quite. Even better, he told me, and I quote, *I don't normally like women who are taller than me, but the way you wear those heels is just so sexy.*"

He'd heard some bad lines in his life, but that was horrible. "He's got a point, you do look sexy in heels. But you also do those Keds justice, so that's kind of a toss-up. So the two of you are going to make happy, beautiful public appropriateness together?" Why was he pushing this?

Pink crept over her cheeks, and she tucked a loose strand of hair behind her ear.

"Large green tea, room for cream?" A voice carried over the crowd, and someone behind the counter held a cup in her direction.

She was on her feet in an instant. "I should go."

His disappointment grew. Would this be the last time they talked? Was high-heels guy waiting for her at home?

The corner of her mouth tugged up, and then the smile vanished again so quickly he wasn't sure he'd seen it. "And nothing happened," she said as she turned away. "Like actual nothing, not the pretend nothing that's really something with us. I'll see you Monday. At least wear a clean T-shirt."

Really something? A wave of relief washed over him, and he wasn't sure if it was related to the fact she wasn't quitting or that she hadn't gone home with another man. He didn't fight his smile. "Yes, ma'am."

Kenzie poured milk and honey into her tea, stirred it all together, and dropped the stick into the trash. She wasn't going to turn around. There was no reason to head back to the table and sit and chat. Scott wasn't on the clock, and it would just ruin the mood if she gave him a hard time for the high tops that looked like they were only staying on thanks to an act of God.

She sipped her tea as she headed home. Why had she even come here? She knew the answer, but she was loathe to admit it. She'd spent the last twelve hours reminding herself she was done with this job. That she was resigning on Monday. But still she'd convinced herself it wouldn't hurt to swing by the coffee shop. It would be the perfect reminder of why she needed to quit.

And instead she'd all but said she was staying on. It was the right thing to do. She could teach that jackass Hank Cartee that Scott was a better man and prove herself at the same time. As long as she and Scott kept their hands off each other moving forward.

She navigated the familiar route, finding herself home much sooner than she wanted. She trudged up the steps, trying to figure out how to approach things from here on out.

Her phone chimed, and she pulled up the new

email from her boss, Greta. There was a URL and a note: *Please tell me this isn't what it looks like.*

Ill-ease crawled through her, and she clicked the link. Her stomach flipped in on itself when she saw the website. Maybe she should have resigned after all.

Scott looked up from his work when a shadow crossed his office. Kenzie stood in the doorway wearing slacks, a matching cream jacket, and a dark shirt buttoned all the way to the top. Did it make her head ache to pull her hair back that tight?

Still, she was there. He hid his smile. He was only relieved she was back because it meant more fun and games, right? He nodded to the chair across from his desk. "Have a seat."

Her expression didn't change. She strolled the short distance to the padded leather, set her laptop bag next to her on the ground, and perched—he couldn't think of a better word for it—with her legs crossed. "Mr. McAllister."

Not this again. He kept his tone pleasant, trying to figure out what he was up against. "Good morning. You look nice."

Her right eye twitched. That was new. She took a deep breath. "Why do you have so many issues?"

The sharp edge in her question sliced through him, and his curiosity shifted to hurt. "Excuse me?"

"I mean publicly, in general." She maintained her straight-backed posture, expression flat. "You're not in a high-profile industry, not as far as executives are concerned. You're not some big-shot Hollywood celebrity. You're a metaphorical suit. Why do I have to worry about things like photos of you in compromising positions showing up on websites? What's so special about your personal life that it's public enough to make your investors nervous?"

She was only just asking these questions? "Shouldn't you already know that? Isn't that why you're here?"

"You'd think that. I certainly did." She managed to pull a manila folder from her laptop bag without bending over and rested it in her lap. "I know it happens, but I want to know why. People care about actors, politicians, public faces. But you're just a software developer. Why does anyone care how you spend your weekends?"

Just? His eyes narrowed at the accusation and the disdain for his job. What had happened between Saturday and now? Had thinking about the situation with Cartee really soured her this much?

He shouldn't go on the defensive, but he couldn't help it. He hadn't done anything to deserve this hostility. "Maybe if you'd paid attention to our company, instead of just harping on what a fuckup I am, you'd know that."

"Maybe if you were taking this seriously, instead of using a couple of stolen kisses as an excuse to not do what you're supposed to, I might have time for things like that."

The honest accusation caught him off-guard, but he recovered quickly. This wasn't about them, it was about his company, and that was more important than almost anything. She opened her mouth, but he cut her off. "When you took this job, did you look at all into how we've built our public image?"

She glared at him. "Of course. Stop trying to change the subject."

A growl slipped out before he could stop it, and he clenched his jaw, forcing his temper back under control. "I'm giving you answers. Consider listening. Bad press almost destroyed us when we started out, and we learned from that. We've used every public moment since as publicity—if it's going to happen anyway, we're going to control it. Besides, keeping our antics exposed to the public eye reminds the fans we're just like them. A side effect is we have a handful of obsessive fans who like to post pictures of us on their Tumblrs. Do I get to know where the third degree is coming from?"

She pulled something from the folder and slid it across his desk. It came to a stop at the edge. He glanced at the printed photos, meaning to dismiss them. He bit back a curse when he saw what they were, not wanting to show how much this was getting under his skin. It was the two of them from dinner, tucked in the back corner of the restaurant looking very cozy right before Cartee interrupted them. How the hell had those gone public? No, better question, why did they exist?

"Explain again." Her icy tone cut through his shock. "Why you have paparazzi-like stalkers posting things like this to gaming forums."

He fumbled for a response, knowing she expected a good one. He couldn't find anything but the truth. "I don't know. This has never happened outside of things like conventions, magazine interviews, stuff like that."

She gritted her teeth, eyes hard. "That's not

good enough. Maybe you could have been a little more up front with me about just how deep and fucked up this fan obsession was. It might have been nice to know before my boss found these pictures. I told you when you hired me it had to be clear you had done so because of my professional skills. Now I have to reassure my employer that I'm actually doing my job instead of playing some executive's afternoon distraction."

He didn't like the baseless accusations, but he'd also never meant to get her in trouble. His tone was as solid and emotionless as hers. "It's never happened before, I swear to you. And it won't happen again."

"Good." Her angry mask didn't budge. "Because it can't. Whatever fucked-up game we're playing has to stop. It doesn't matter how good you may or not be with your fingers. We're not a couple, this is a professional relationship, and anything else ends now."

A new wave of anger and hurt surged through him. "I'm sorry, Miss Carter. I've always been under the impression you were a willing participant."

She flinched, but didn't look away. "That's not my point."

He rolled his eyes. "Fine. If we're done, then I assume you have some new hoops for me to jump through? Things to make you and your career look good?"

She opened her folder, and scanned the papers still inside. "You've got a DECA meeting tomorrow at a local high school. Should be simple enough. Even you should be able to avoid compromising pictures."

He clenched his fist, resisting the urge to slam it

into his desk. Instead, he stood and moved to crouch in front of her. He stopped when they were at eye level, never touching her. His voice was low. It was the only way he could control his tone. "Be honest. Is this whole pictures thing really such a big deal that you have to storm into my office like the entire world is coming to an end? That you have to insult me?"

Her brows knit together. "This isn't just about what the public may or may not think of you anymore. This puts my entire job at risk. People can't start thinking I sleep with clients."

Every word devoured him more. He stared at her, keeping his gaze locked on hers. Why couldn't he drop this? He felt terrible that it might have gotten her in trouble, but his ego wouldn't let him just walk away. "Did you enjoy it? Any of that horrific intimacy that you think is going to crush your soul? Did you get to prove to yourself that you're not frigid?"

Her expression wavered again, uncertainty slipping in. She leaned toward him, and then her back went rigid again. "It doesn't matter."

His head swam at the light flower of her perfume. This was about proving a point. He wasn't going to get sucked down the hole of how intoxicating she was. "It's a yes or no question."

"Yes. I enjoyed it." Her reply was almost lost in the hum of the air conditioner it was so quiet. "But it still doesn't matter."

Victory. Concession. So why did he still feel like a wounded dog? He leaned in, face inches from hers, struggling to ignore her scent and the warmth she radiated. "Sometimes, that's the only thing that matters. Maybe you've got some serious soul-searching to do if you're willing to surrender that for something as basic and superficial as what other people think of you."

She didn't pull away, but uncertainty flickered in her eyes. Her voice wasn't as strong as it had been. "What aren't you getting? This is a bit more serious than whether or not a couple of people like the way I hold myself in public."

He knew that, so why couldn't he admit it? Her words cut too deeply to ignore. He hated thinking he'd been the only one having fun. "I understand." He didn't move. "Are we done?"

"I suppose so."

He leaned in, mouth near her ear. He forced his voice to remain steady, despite the almost overwhelming urge to kiss her long, slender neck. "I'm sorry to hear it."

She inhaled sharply, but didn't move.

Disappointment mingled with his anger, and he took his seat behind his desk again. "I have work to do." He turned back to his computer, not able to look at her anymore. "I'll call you after school tomorrow."

She hesitated at the edge of her chair.

"Is that all?"

She didn't answer, and seconds later his office door swung shut as she disappeared through it.

A sharp pain gnawed his chest. Why did her dismissal—her ability to write the entire thing off so easily—hurt so much?

chapter eleven

Kenzie stripped off her suit and draped the jacket, top, and skirt next to the other outfits she needed to drop off at the dry cleaner in the morning. She'd spent the day catching up on paperwork, making sure everything was going okay, getting behind-the-scenes things like press releases in place for Scott and his company. Her eyes ached from scanning so many emails and filing them. She couldn't believe she'd let her inbox get over ten messages.

She grabbed a fitted T-shirt from her top drawer and yanked it on. She was reaching for a pair of shorts when her phone rang. The professional chime told her it was work-related. She rolled her eyes and slid her earpiece on before answering. "This is Mackenzie."

"How's my favorite mistress?" Scott's snide greeting added a layer to her exhaustion.

At least that would make it easier not to fall into bad habits. She set her phone on the nightstand and flopped back on her bed, making sure the motion didn't jar her earpiece loose. The conversation from the day before still echoed in her thoughts—he hadn't even bothered to deny her accusations he wasn't taking this serious—and she wasn't sure if she was furious or just frustrated. "Something tells me you're not a bowing, scraping, boot-kissing kind of guy."

"You'd be surprised."

She didn't have the patience for whatever he was up to. So why did she want to keep him on the phone, letting his voice tickle her ear? "I usually am with you. How was your thing?"

"Fantastic." His voice went flat. "I wore a shirt and a tie—a nice shirt, like almost no stains—and now not a single member of DECA wants to be a computer programmer when they grow up because I was so dry and professional they were all either passed out or threatening to stab their eardrums out when I finished lecturing."

Was he serious? He couldn't be. Please let him be joking. "How did it really go?"

He snorted. "Great. Like it usually does. I swear on my series bible I didn't do anything that would piss anyone off." He paused. "Well, anyone in the industry. I may have broken a few mothers' hearts when their kids went home and said they wanted to play video games for a living, but those kids weren't going to be doctors anyway."

"Sounds like fun." The corner of her mouth twitched, and she forced a frown back in place. She wasn't enjoying this beyond a professional level. He'd been an ass, and she was still pissed off at him.

"So." His voice abruptly dropped in volume. "I'm sorry about the pictures that got out, and I'm sorry about what I said yesterday."

The apology caught her off guard. She wanted to believe it was because she didn't think he was capable of admitting when he was wrong—that was easier than admitting he might not be the only one regretting what they'd said. "Don't worry about it."

"I am worried about it. I promised you we'd keep the professional and physical separate, and I violated that trust."

She appreciated the unique combination of conceit and self-effacing humor he radiated without trying. Was she actually enjoying this conversation? Crap. "It's done and over, and as long as we're more careful about where we are when we step from one role to the other—as long as the line doesn't blur again—it's all good."

"I'm glad to hear it." His voice returned to normal, a hint of familiar joking sliding back in. "You know what else I'm glad to hear?"

She furrowed her brow. "No?"

"That I can finally take off this freaking tie. For the record, these things drive me nuts."

He'd actually dressed up; she was impressed. Still, she had to give him a hard time for complaining about something most people did by default. "Poor baby had to be professional for a couple hours today? Too bad I'm not there, or I could help you into something less restrictive." Damn it, why had she said that?

His throaty laugh sent a pleasant tremor through her, erasing the lingering strands of her irritation. "So not to change the subject, because I could listen to you talk all night about undressing me, but are you bringing anyone tomorrow?"

The way he'd slid into the flirting and out again without a pause heightened the tingles moving over her skin. No reason to let him know that. "I was thinking I'd invite that guy I met at the bar the other night."

"I, uh…" He trailed off. "High-heels guy? Because, really?"

So he wasn't completely in control of the conversation. She smirked even though he couldn't see it. "No, not really. My sister."

"The twin?"

"She's the only sister I've got." She cringed when more of the bar conversation filtered through her thoughts. "You're not one of those guys with creepy twin fantasies, are you?"

"Maybe." He quickly added, "No, not really. I'm kind of vanilla like that. Incest doesn't do it for me."

The reassurance settled deep. Should she be enjoying this conversation so much? "Vanilla. Right. Because sex in a dressing room is tame."

"Exactly."

She paused, waiting for more, disappointment and embarrassment flitting through her when she realized they were suffering awkward silence syndrome. She needed something witty to say.

"So." His voice startled her. "What are you wearing?"

The question caught her off guard. "T-shirt and panties." Crap, why had she blurted that out? Why had he asked? She struggled to correct herself. "I just got home, and you called before I finished changing."

"Not at all what I meant, but it sounds a lot more fun than what I'm wearing. Maybe I should strip down so we match. Only seems fair, right? Less awkward?"

Fantastic logic. She wanted to be bothered by it, but she couldn't keep the grin from her face as teasing fantasies tripped through her thoughts. "Yes. You stripping down to your boxers so we can have a less awkward phone conversation sounds completely reasonable."

"You're not convincing me." A hint of teasing wove into his voice. "If you'd prefer, I could tell you if I was there, I'd strip your shirt off." His voice dropped an octave. "Run my lips over your neck. Slide my hands up your sides."

She was grateful her bedroom window was open a crack because the flush flooding her entire body was raising the temperature by several degrees. She had been the one to demand they tone things down. She should change the subject. Except she didn't want to. It wasn't like anyone could take pictures of this. "Really?" Her question came out sultry and breathy. "Then what?"

There was a long pause. "Hello?" she asked.

"Sorry, I was trying to decide if this is a good idea." Something unrecognizable tinged his response. Disappointment, maybe?

She sighed. She didn't want the conversation to end, but his pause had given her time to think. After the lecture she'd given him the day before, she didn't have any right to play like this.

"Then again." His smooth tone beat back her weak hesitation. "You're still here, I'm still here, and no one's watching."

"I don't have anywhere else to be." One more time wouldn't hurt, right? Especially since they weren't even in the same room. Anticipation was already pulsing through her at how wicked the entire thing was.

"Is that an invitation?" He didn't sound upset, just hesitant.

Screw it. She could go back to being good tomorrow. "Just this once."

"Or this fourth time?" he countered. "Not that I'm counting. Promise me I won't regret it in the morning. Or even better, that you won't."

"I've never regretted it." The honesty slipped out before she realized it probably wasn't the best thing to tell him. "And this would be one hundred percent private."

"You make a convincing case, Miss Carter." The way her name rolled off his tongue made her tingle. The professional, mocking tone he usually used was gone, replaced with a heavy seduction. "So where were we?"

"You were describing how you'd ravish me if you were here instead of miles away."

His laugh was warm and deep. She closed her eyes, imagining him in the room with her. His voice had dropped an octave. "You do this gasping, moaning thing when I nibble your earlobe that kind of drives me wild, so I'd probably do a lot of that."

She did something that drove him wild. Her entire body tingled with not quite visualized fantasies and she moaned.

"Just like that. I love that sound."

Heat crawled over her, and she ran her hand up her stomach. "Did you make yourself match yet?"

"I'm lying on my bed in a pair of boxers, nothing else."

The image popped into her head, taunting her, and she sighed.

"It's not fair if I'm the only one saying what I'm thinking." There was a hint of command in his teasing. "At least reassure me this is turning you on as much as it is me."

She was turning him on? She hesitated, having trouble forming the words. "I'm tingling, and aroused, and aching with the thoughts of what you can do with your fingers."

"Just my fingers?"

"Not just. Everything else too." She pushed her shirt aside, brushing the bottom of her own breasts with her fingertips.

His throaty voice filled her thoughts. "I'm hard just thinking about sucking on your nipples. How they feel against my tongue, and the way you squirm under me."

She hesitated. The conversation was screaming over every nerve ending, but saying those kinds of things out loud was a line she didn't know if she could cross.

"We'll have to work on the whole telling me what you're thinking thing." His voice was heavy. "Since I'm not there, are you touching yourself?"

"Yes." Her reply was breathy, soft. She squeezed her breast, gasping when she pinched her own tender skin.

His breathing was ragged. "Tell me those

moans are real."

"Very." A hot ache called for her attention between her legs.

His moan tickled her ear. "You know I'm stroking myself harder every time you say something new, right?"

The confession increased her arousal another notch. That she could have that impact on him, just by talking, sent her into overdrive. "I do now."

"Tell me what you're doing to yourself. What you'd want me to do if I was there," he ordered.

The outside world seemed to fall away, and she let herself sink into the sensation. It was as if only they existed, making it safe to say things she would never dream of vocalizing. "I do have this fantasy."

"I like the sound of that. Details?"

With her eyes closed, she could almost feel his warm breath, his lips vibrating against her skin with each rumbling word. She licked her lips. "Of you pinning my arms over my head, holding me in place while you pound inside me."

His soft groan filtered into her ear. "There's no way you'd let me get away with that."

"I would." Her body tingled and screamed for more everywhere her hand touched. Her stomach, her thighs. "Especially when you growl. I'd do pretty much anything with that sound rolling through my skin."

His voice shifted, the same irresistible growl running through it. "Anything?"

She arched her back, a whimper slipping out before she could stop it. "Drop to my knees, wrap a hand around your shaft, take you in my mouth."

"I like that a lot. What about putting on a show?"

She hadn't thought it could get any warmer in the room until he said that. Her "What?" was barely a squeak.

"On your back, spread wide open, showing me how you really like it."

Her heart hammered in her chest, making it difficult to hear. "I couldn't."

"No?" Teasing disappointment ran through his question. "You're almost doing it now, right?"

She swallowed. "It's not the same. No one's watching."

"Would it be so bad if I was?" Seduction lined his coercion. "I bet you're lying on your comforter right now. Humor me. Tell me if it would be such a horrible thing if I were in the room with you."

She let the thought flit through her mind, and the heat between her legs screamed in response. "Maybe."

"Maybe it would be a bad thing?"

Her voice was soft. "Maybe it would be okay."

His sigh sent tingles through her. His voice was coaxing, but didn't leave room for argument. "Then it's a shame I'm not there."

"Very much so." She breathed the words, almost able to feel him hovering over her.

"So you'll have to tell me about it instead. I can't forget how good you tasted in the dressing room. The scent of your perfume—just the memory of that screws with my head. What would it take to get you gasping like that again?"

Okay, she could do the talking. No public

audience. Still, she couldn't get the image of him watching her out of her thoughts, and it heightened the moment to an intensity she wouldn't have thought possible. "You're doing a pretty good job already."

"Touch yourself."

She moved her hand down, dipping between her own folds. "I'm so wet right now." She glided along her slit, lightly brushing. "My fingers are soaked."

"Put them inside you."

She did as she was told, squirming under her own touch, pumping in and out, and making sure he heard her moans and sighs. "It's not the same as you being here," she managed between gasps. "But it's not bad."

"You're still imagining me watching?"

"Yes." She couldn't get rid of the thought, and it was making her mind short-circuit.

"Play with your clit." That hungry growl had invaded his voice again. "Show me how you like it."

She moved her hand back up, gasping in shock and pleasure when she brushed the swollen nub. "I won't last much longer if you make me do this."

"Good." His breath was heavy against the receiver. "Rub it hard and fast, I want to hear you come."

She did, stroking in small circles, feeling her climax build inside. She tried to keep the motion slow, but desire won out. As she peaked, she didn't try and hold back the cries. Her hips thrust against her hands until her own touch was too much, and she shuddered as she pulled away.

His breath was heavy in her ear, and she kept

her eyes closed, imagining the heat brushing her skin.

"Are you close?" Her voice was soft, coaxing. "Knowing how wet you made me. How hard I came imagining you watch me? How swollen and sensitive my nipples are from thinking about your tongue flicking over them? Pretending I'm there with you, stroking, sucking, pleading with my eyes for you to finish."

"God, yes." His familiar grunts greeted her, stretching on for several seconds before nothing but pants filled the line.

She opened her eyes, her entire body relaxing. She licked her lips, a soft smile playing on her face, and waited for him to be able to talk again. The breeze from the window brushed her flushed skin, and she watched the patterns dance on the ceiling. Her voice was still breathy. "You're a horrible influence on me."

"If I thought you were doing anything you didn't want to, I wouldn't ask." The deep grumble was still there, soft and seductive. "But if you're complaining…"

"No." She assured him. "Most certainly not."

He laughed—he was doing a lot of it that night, and it sounded wonderful. "Me too. I've never done anything like that before."

"Masturbation? Really? The tail's been that good for that long in your life?" It felt good to be the one doing the teasing.

"Phone sex. I can assure you I've been beating off since before I was a teenager."

"Typical guy. So, when was your first time?"

"I—" He paused. "You're serious."

The hesitation caught her attention. "I am now."

"You'll laugh." The uncertainty in his tone was out of character. He had so many layers.

"I won't," she assured him. "But now you have to tell me, or I'll make something up about it being with a Sears catalog."

"No. That would be normal." He gave a nervous laugh. "It was a D & D monster compendium."

Her jaw dropped, and she was glad he couldn't see her shock. "Dungeons and Dragons? You jerked off to a book with Cthulhu in it?"

"There was this drow queen, and she was hot, and I was young, and it wasn't like my parents believed in things like Sears catalogs, and they hated that I gamed, so it was already taboo, and I wasn't allowed to have an internet connection in my room at that age."

A snort of laugher slipped out. "I'm sorry." She bit back her amusement. "I can't help it. A black-skinned, dominant elf in a chainmail bikini."

"Yes." Indignation rang heavy in his voice. "You can't laugh that hard if you know what I'm talking about."

She shook her head. "Riley plays. A drow, really?"

"What about you? Is this your first time?"

She shouldn't let him redirect the conversation, but she didn't want to ruin the moment. "No to the masturbation, yes to the phone sex."

"So another first for me." He didn't sound smug the way she'd expected.

The heat that had finally started to dissipate from her body flooded back in. "Maybe." She swallowed the rest of her comment, not wanting to inflate his ego by telling him just his voice was sending chills through her. On second thought, screw reservation. "It's a shame you're not here."

"So you could tease me to my face?"

She winced at the hint of seriousness in his joke. "So I could curl up against you and fall asleep." Her words were faint, even to her own ears, but she felt a flood of warm relief having said it out loud.

"I like that idea."

Another pause hung between them, but this time she didn't feel any panic, as though she needed to fill the void. She'd never felt so exposed before, but at the same time she felt completely comfortable and safe.

"So." He broke the silence again, voice still low and deep. "Now will you answer my question?"

She hadn't answered enough? Her brow furrowed. "Which was?"

"What are you wearing?" he asked again. "To the investor dinner tomorrow night," he added.

Oh. Her blush deepened when she realized the last half hour had been built off that one misunderstanding. And she didn't regret it for a second. "Why?"

"Maybe. Why. Maybe. Why. You need some new words," he teased. "It's a surprise. I don't need details or anything, just a color. Black? Red?"

Red at an investor dinner? Tacky. The vagueness made her curious, but he wasn't going to spill unless he wanted to, so there was no reason to push. "Yes, black."

"Sounds stunning. See you tomorrow night."

She turned her head to the side, knocking her earpiece out, and stared at the phone on her nightstand. What was that about? Any of it. Her pulse sped up every time another snippet of the conversation replayed in her head, bringing a new revelation with it. She was falling for him. The thought warmed every inch of her until she remembered this was supposed to be a strictly physical relationship. Damn it.

chapter twelve

Kenzie stood with her sister just out of most people's view at the edge of the room, watching guests mingle pre-dinner. Some were already staking out tables, others gathered near the bar or in small clumps, chatting and gossiping.

Boredom was already sinking into Riley's expression as she smoothed invisible wrinkles from a red dress that was almost too short to be acceptable. "Ritzy. Dull."

Kenzie rolled her eyes and handed her keys to her sister. "I'm glad I trust you to behave. Hold my keys until after dinner?"

Riley dropped them in a satin handbag that matched her dress and let the wristlet dangle. "Why aren't you carrying a purse? You have five billion black ones."

"None looked right." Kenzie had fidgeted in front of the mirror for hours as it was. She'd tried to tell herself it was because this was an extraordinarily important night for a client. Part of her knew it was because she wanted to look good for Scott.

"You know," Scott's smooth voice right next to her ear startled her, "I don't usually like women who wear all black, but the way you do it is just so sexy."

A warm tremor ran through her, and her pulse increased. She bit back a smile and spun to face him. "You're not going to let that go, are you?"

"I might once it gets old. If it gets old." He was wearing a suit she'd never seen before. An actual tuxedo, bow tie, cummerbund, the works.

She ran her fingers along the edge of his lapels "Is this real silk?"

He shrugged. "You really do look amazing. Is this Riley?"

Riley's gaze raked over him, appraising, a smirk replacing her boredom, and she stuck out her hand. "Are you the wallet?"

Kenzie had to fight the urge to slap her forehead.

Scott just laughed and returned the handshake. "I suppose. Do you mind if I borrow your dinner date for a moment?"

Riley shrugged, mischief still dancing on her face. "Suit yourself. I'll go find another one."

Kenzie grabbed her sister's fingers. "Not any of the board members, please."

Riley rolled her eyes and shook her head. "You mean those old guys? I had my eye on that really cute waiter. Besides, you just said you trust me."

"Fine." Kenzie let her go.

Scott chuckled. "You were right, only physically identical."

Had she just been insulted? Kenzie studied him, still a little breathless at how incredible he looked.

"I mean it in the best way possible." He grasped her wrist loosely and tugged.

She hissed softly at the tender contact—this wasn't the time or place to lose herself in his touch—and allowed herself to be pulled even farther out of anyone's line of sight.

He leaned against a pillar and dropped his hands into his pockets, toe tapping. "Thank you for coming tonight."

She ducked her head. "Of course. I couldn't pass up a chance to see you looking good." She realized how that sounded. "With your peers," she quickly added. Professional. She had to keep this professional. "All my hard work paying off and all that."

His fidgeting increased. "Right." He pulled his hand from his pocket. A small black box rested in his palm. "This is for you. I hear corsages are tacky at grown-up parties, so I hope this will do instead."

Her curiosity spiked as she took it from him. The velvet was soft against her fingers. She gasped at what was inside, and her heart hammered in her ears. A delicate violet made of gems and surrounded by a smattering of diamonds hung from a silver chain. "It's beautiful."

"I know you don't wear chains often, but I saw it and thought of you." He took the box from her and pulled the necklace out. "May I?"

She frowned and took a step back. Every inch of her was screaming yes, take it. But she didn't know how to interpret the gesture. Was she setting herself up to fall even harder by accepting? The unpleasant thought made her chest ache, and she pushed it aside. "It's stunning, and I love it. But you know I can't take gifts from clients."

The corner of his mouth pulled up, and he didn't look deterred. "It's true. But if we're playing by all the rules now, there's probably a more serious one we've broken." He didn't back down, but he didn't step closer. "Besides, your contract says bonuses are allowed."

People tended to conveniently overlook that clause. "You took the time to read my contract that closely?" She didn't know what to think of that.

He looked confused. "I always do." He held his hand out again, the flower sparkling against his palm. "Will you wear it, or do I need to pout?" He stuck his lower lip out.

She bit back a laugh. "Stick to puppy-dog eyes. The pouting doesn't work for you." She turned so her back was to him, grateful her hair was already pulled up. "And it's gorgeous. Of course I'll wear it."

She barely felt the pendant rest against her chest. Her breath caught when his fingers brushed her neck while doing up the clasp. His thumbs grazed her back, and she closed her eyes at the feeling of his breath on her skin. His touch lingered after the chain dropped into place, and her pulse increased.

The contact snapped abruptly, and her eyes flew open.

"Let me see." A tremor ran through his voice.

She spun, forcing aside her disappointment that they were in such a public place.

He had stepped back to rest against the pillar again, putting a more casual valley between them. "You look amazing. Don't disappear before I get to introduce you around. Show everyone the woman who whipped me into shape."

She fingered the flower at the base of her throat, wanting the moment back. "Of course. I'm always up for networking."

Scott was going to shoot himself. Or stab himself. Would a salad fork do the trick, or would he need to upgrade to a steak knife? Even Kenzie's smile from earlier at the gift wasn't enough to keep his mood light. Not that he'd given it to her to make her smile. It was a bonus, just like he'd said. She'd done a good job despite the grief he gave her. And he'd give her a thousand more if he could get the same reaction every time.

He'd give her a million more to get her to open up again the way she had on the phone. Not the intimate details—though he wouldn't complain—but the side of her she kept so tightly tucked away. He pushed the thought aside. Now wasn't the time.

He hated these parties; they reminded him of bits of his past he'd rather not remember. At least they were only once a year. And Cartee had been too busy to attend. He ignored his aching cheeks from a fake smile and shook another investor's hand. He smiled and kissed the man's wife on the cheek, letting the drivel that was small talk leak from his mouth while he struggled to look like he was interested in the conversation.

His gaze flitted around the room, occasionally falling on Kenzie. Every time she was laughing and chatting with someone else. He couldn't imagine being as at ease as she looked.

He pointed toward the bar when asked where it

was. What he wouldn't give to be able to join them. A straight bourbon would pretty much solve his entire evening. Which was why he knew he needed to stay away. He smiled at the couple as they wandered off. "Enjoy the evening. It was marvelous to see you."

He drifted from group to group, resisting the urge to check his watch every few seconds. The men in suits, the women in satin, the rows of flowers decorating the tables, and the well-dressed bartender serving up free drinks. It was all so much pomp. He sighed, gaze falling on Kenzie again. She was talking to an older gentleman. Her fingers rested at the base of her throat, fiddling with the small pendant.

She caught his eye, and her smile grew. She waved and nodded for him to join them.

Reprieve or more of the same boredom? He hoped for the former as he wove through the pockets of people, nodding and responding when appropriate. A few moments later, he finally reached his destination.

He recognized her companion now that he was closer. Grant Lent had been one of their earliest investors in the new venture and was one of the few Scott enjoyed talking to.

"Scott, my good man." Grant shook his hand and clapped him on the shoulder. "Your girl was just telling me all sorts of glowing things about you."

Kenzie coughed.

"My girl?" Scott didn't know how to interpret that, and the ripple that went through him was disconcerting and reassuring at the same time.

Grant frowned and paused for a moment. "I

forget that's not appropriate these days. This amazing young lady was talking you up." He leaned in, voice a stage whisper. "I don't think she realizes she doesn't need to sell me, I already bought in."

He smiled back, the expression genuine and not nearly so painful as it had been before. "She's good at her job."

"Oh I know." Grant knocked back a swallow from a snifter. "We had her on a year or so ago. I think I gave you her name. She and I were reminiscing, and she was telling me how much potential she sees in you boys and your future. She's got me curious about what you're up to."

So that's how Zach found her. Scott felt smug at the string of compliments, but had she meant it or was she just doing her job? "You'll get a peek at that after dinner."

"I'm not worried." Grant winked at Kenzie. "I am hoping you'll tell me something that you're not going to share with everyone else."

The conversation was always the same, and Scott didn't mind the friendly joking. "No, I still don't pick up strippers when I'm in Vegas."

Kenzie frowned, lips drawing into a fine line. Scott bit back a retort. There was no way she could get on his case for that comment. This was a good old boy. He was playing the part she wanted him to.

"Not that a young man like you needs to pay for it, right?" Grant elbowed him. "But seriously, tell me what's going on with Cartee. The actual deal, not the political bullshit we hear in board meetings."

Kenzie shook her head so slightly it was almost difficult to tell, her eyes growing wide as she stared

Scott down.

He turned away from the silent plea to keep his mouth shut. "Same old stuff. He can't get laid, so he takes it out on me. He wants to take us in a different direction, tamer games, more commercial titles, and the fact it's my company and I'm not interested makes him bawl like a newb with more ego than sense who's spent the last hour being camped. Miserable, but status quo, like any good long-term relationship."

Grant frowned and went to take another swallow, pausing when he realized his snifter was empty. "Time for a refill." He studied Scott for a moment. "I know sometimes you have to make a deal with the devil to keep your soul, but make sure you haven't signed away more than you bargained for."

"Of course. We're always careful," Scott assured him. He wished he felt as confident as he sounded. He stared at the older man's retreating back, not liking the ominous warning.

"I can't believe you told him that. Especially about someone you both work with." Kenzie's growl was closer than it should be, her low voice near his ear short-circuiting his thoughts.

She was telling him how to do his job? Her assumption, combined with the brain drain that was his evening, killed the buzz of want, and he spun to face her. "There are some things I still have control of around here, and that's not your call."

She stepped back, wide eyes narrowing as irritation replaced surprise. "Of course. I apologize, Mr. McAllister. I should go find a seat before dinner begins."

Damn it, why had he snapped at her like that? And why couldn't he find the apology to take the words back? Scott's fake, painful smile was back. Because this was still his, that was why. She couldn't corrupt everything. "Enjoy the rest of the evening."

He turned away before she could, fury and ill ease pumping through him. Grant's ominous words about Cartee hit harder than he expected. He should be reassured that someone agreed with him. Instead he wondered if he was really in over his head this time. And then Kenzie, assumptive, obnoxious, telling him how to run his own company. And still he felt bad about snapping at her.

He drifted through dinner, thoughts a jumble, the steak tasting like sawdust. He was mechanical through his presentation about their upcoming game. Normally it might have been enough to make him smile, but these people didn't want to know details. They weren't interested in how he and his team had come up with the ideas, the engine, the shading on the characters. They just wanted to know how much it would make them.

And his attention drifted several times to the woman in black, sitting next to her mirror image but in a red dress. He told himself he didn't notice or care when Riley vanished halfway through the meal, making Kenzie's frown deepen.

As the evening wound down, some people stayed at their tables, sipping coffee and picking at barely touched crème brûlée. Others broke into groups similar to before, or said their goodbyes and took the next forty minutes to make it to the exit.

Scott struggled to keep his eyes from drifting

shut. His face felt frozen in a smile. He stood next to Zach and Rae, keeping his attention turned from how happy they looked together, and shook more hands, accepted more compliments, kissed more asses.

He stood straighter, no longer so exhausted, when Kenzie approached. He was still upset about what she'd done with Grant, but boredom and too many phony words had taken the edge off. She shook Zach's hand. "You were great tonight. Thank you for having me."

Zach played the roles as well as she did, returning the enthusiasm and her quick hug. "I'm glad you made it. Have you met Rae?"

"No, but I've been dying to." Kenzie was almost a foot taller in heels. Statuesque. Scott pushed the thought away. She shook Rae's hand as well. "I've heard a lot about you. Congratulations on the engagement. It's my understanding these two wouldn't be here without you."

Scott hid his surprise. She'd really done her research if she knew Rae had saved their asses. It had never been public knowledge that the shorter woman's business plan had gotten them through their second startup.

Rae's smile was still sincere, but not as bright. "I hear the same about you. But I'm not so big on believing the rumors. I like to find out the truth on my own."

Scott didn't know if he wanted to snarl at her or hug her for the comment. Kenzie had reached him, smile softening, sadness tingeing the blue of her eyes. She shook his hand as she had everyone else's. "You were brilliant. Your investors are lucky people."

The compliment pushed more of his irritation away, and he hated himself for it. She was just playing a role. A part. Doing her job.

She leaned in, giving him a quick hug as she had with Zach, mouth near his ear and voice so low no one else could hear it. "I'm so very sorry about earlier. It wasn't my place, and I would never question your judgment about things like that."

Things like that. The qualifier almost took the edge off the apology, but only almost. He dipped his head in a short bow. "We'll see you in the office again soon, Miss Carter."

The corner of her mouth tugged down for the briefest moment before her smile returned full force. "Enjoy the rest of your evening, all three of you."

He tried not to watch her walk away. The way her dress hugged her curves, dropping to the floor and swishing around her feet with every smooth step. It was a shame she hadn't worn something open-backed, but the high collar had its own seductive allure.

An elbow landed in his side and he frowned, yanking his attention back to his immediate surroundings. Rae stood next to him, lips pursed, tiny smile on her face. Her voice was low. "She's kind of formal and stuck up."

Not when no one was looking. The thought sent a pulse through Scott, waking him up even more. He greeted the next wave of well-wishers and waited until they were gone to reply. "That's what we pay her for." He nodded at Zach. "So's he when he thinks someone is watching."

She glanced at Zach, smile growing. "I didn't say it was a bad thing. Doesn't it drive you nuts though?"

He both adored and loathed how well Rae knew him sometimes. "It's not supposed to make me happy. It's supposed to make Cartee happy."

Smile pasted in place, she turned away to make small talk with someone Zach had introduced her to. It was a silly formality. Even though she wasn't officially an employee, she'd been on the payroll as a consultant for several years, and she knew the investors as well as anyone.

She broke away as quickly as she could, even less comfortable with the pomp than Scott. "I heard about that. You really threatened to deck him?"

Scott shrugged. "He insulted one of my people."

She hid her snicker behind her hand. "You're such an alpha dog sometimes."

"I'm not." The term had always bothered him. Something about the idea of throwing his weight around just because he could didn't feel right. "He was being an ass."

"Hank's always an ass," she reminded him. "But you are completely putting me off-topic. You should make sure she gets home safe."

Scott raised an eyebrow, struggling to hide how enticing the idea was. "If only."

A knowing look flashed in Rae's eyes. "Don't tell me you're worried about what people will think?"

"Am I ever?" He rolled his eyes, unable to keep his smile hidden. The conversation should have bugged the hell out of him. So why had it erased the ache in his cheeks instead?

His phone buzzed, and his hand flew to his pocket out of instinct. He ignored Zach's dirty look for taking the call and stepped away from the group to read the new message from Kenzie.

Stepping out for the night. You really were brilliant. I'm sorry again.

She couldn't leave.

Wait, why not? The impulse confounded him. He pocketed his phone and took his place next to Rae. He kept his voice low as he bent to whisper in her ear. "If I don't make it back, tell everyone I had to talk to Japan before the markets opened."

"Japan. Got it."

He stepped away before Zach could stop him. With people slowly trickling out, it was much easier to sift through the crowds than it had been earlier. He was only stopped three times before he found Kenzie on a bench near the coat check, elbows on her knees, and face buried in her hands. That seemed out of place.

He slid onto the seat next to her, stopping just short of brushing her arm with his. "I'm glad I caught you."

She looked up, eyes wide and rimmed with red.

His chest ached in response. "Are you all right?"

Her lips were tight. "My sister took off, supposedly with a busboy. She's got my keys. Even if I call a cab, I can't get into my condo. Not that I want to go home. I'm so furious with her I don't even want to see her tonight."

The frustration and waver in her voice ate at him. "I can take you home."

"So you have an excuse to take off? Were you listening to anything I said?"

He stood and offered her a hand, refusing to consider what he was about to say. Part of him knew that was a bad idea, and he told it to shut up. "So I can rescue the maiden in distress. Besides, I never said *your* home."

Her mouth twisted in indecision. "I can't put you out like that. Not on a big night like this. I'll just go hang out at Denny's or something until Riley answers my messages."

"I have a guest bedroom. Better coffee than Denny's. Hopefully better company than whatever's on your phone." He tried to keep the pleading from his voice, but he knew it was going to hurt if she turned him down.

A smile leaked in and she took his hand, letting him pull her to her feet. "How can I say no to an offer like that?"

He forced his attention from the way her hand nestled against his, warm, soft, clinging for longer than it should. "Come on. I've already made my excuses, let's bail."

chapter thirteen

The entire ride to Scott's place was tense. Kenzie spent most of it staring out the window, and he struggled to think of a way to start up a conversation. It took focus to keep his eyes on the road instead of tracing the curve of her neck, studying the way her dress hugged her shape, watching the disappointed heave of her chest every time she sighed. She was out of the car the moment he pulled into his parking spot, waiting next to the door with her hands folded together.

Indecision ripped through him. He didn't know if he wanted to force her further away, or do whatever it took to make her smile.

But he did know. He was falling for her. Wanted her desperately and not just because the sex was incredible. He was struggling to keep from wrapping her up and comforting her. Except her hesitation when he'd offered her a ride home pretty much cemented for him she didn't feel the same way.

He kept his distance as they made their way to the elevator. He swiped his wallet over the security bar and pressed the button for the top floor.

As they ascended, fantasy taunted him.

Thoughts of bringing the elevator to a stop assaulted him, or even just pulling her close and running his hands over her for a quick, deep kiss before they reached their destination. He could almost feel her pressed against him.

The car glided to a stop, the doors slid open, and he pushed the thoughts aside. He let her step out first, gesturing to the only door on the floor. He forced himself to study the familiar beige walls, the rich silver rug, anything boring and familiar and not her ass, as they crossed the short distance to his door.

He reached around her, careful not to make any contact that could screw further with his head, and opened the door.

She paused just inside, and he had to straighten up and tuck in on himself to slide past without touching her. Her gaze seemed transfixed by the four large-screen TV's lining the wall and the battered micro-suede sectional that might not land him in *Better Homes and Gardens*, but at least it was comfortable.

A smile tugged on her lips. "It's not what I pictured, but I like it. A lot."

He tried not to let the compliment warm him and failed. He nodded toward the closet. "You can leave your shoes in there. I can, I don't know, try and dig you up something more comfortable to change into." *Please let that not be the wrong thing to say.* Maybe she wanted to wear the evening gown for a few more hours.

She shrunk a few inches when she stepped out of her shoes. "That would be nice."

He headed toward his bedroom without another

word and draped his jacket and vest over the back of a chair, happy to be rid of at least one restriction. He yanked open a drawer and sifted through T-shirts until he found a newer one. White, simple, with someone's black graphic on the back.

"I like your room." Her soft voice startled him.

He whirled, surprised to see her lingering in the doorway, gaze on him and nowhere else. He didn't know how much longer he could fake the small talk without sliding into flirting. He handed her the shirt. "You can wear this. I'll dig you up a pair of shorts or something to go with it."

"It's fine, thank you." She took it with a smile and turned her back to him. "Unzip me?"

Oh geez, seriously? The blood rushed from his head to fill his lower extremities.

She glanced over her shoulder at him. "It's hard to reach by myself, and it's not nearly as comfortable as I'm sure it looks. Please?"

He swallowed hard and grabbed her zipper. His pulse screamed as he slid it down the length of her back, the two halves of her dress parting and exposing pale, smooth skin. It took all his restraint not to lean in and trail his lips down her spine. He realized his breathing was shallow. Why was his hammering heart choosing this moment to betray his reluctance to be hurt by her?

She dropped the dress, and it pooled around her feet. Still standing with her back to him, she raised her hands over her head. Every curve was elongated, accented by black lace panties and matching thigh-high stockings. She tugged his shirt over her head, and it dropped into place. Even though she was only a few inches shorter, she was enough thinner that it ended halfway down her thighs, right above her stockings.

She plucked the chopsticks from her hair and shook it loose as she spun to face him.

He struggled to keep his eyes on her face, failing as he traced her figure and the way his shirt hinted at everything that was and wasn't underneath. That was so not any better.

She studied him for a moment and then stepped closer. "I can't believe you didn't yank this off hours ago."

Her fingers worked their way under his tie, brushing his throat. He inhaled sharply.

She gave him a curious look while she loosened the bow. She worked her way down the front of his shirt, undoing each button as she moved, pulling it open when she reached the bottom. "Better?"

"No." His voice barely reached his own ears.

Her bottom lip stuck out. "What's wrong?"

He clenched his hands into fists, fighting back the urge to trace a finger over her pout, or press her against the wall and kiss her until he couldn't breathe, and even then he might not stop. He took a deep breath and tried to compose himself enough to answer. "I'm good. I just need some sleep."

Her frown deepened. "You're not good."

With her still standing in the doorway, he couldn't get around her without touching her. He stepped back into his room, but putting the extra space between them didn't help clear his thoughts. An ache throbbed below his waist. "You're making it really hard to behave myself."

She rested a hand on his chest, and then slid lower to his belt. "You've never complained before."

He grabbed her wrist, her skin almost searing his hand. "You're the one who keeps insisting we put some professional distance between us. If you keep this up, that won't happen. The only thing I can think about right now is how amazing you look in my shirt, and how you'd look even better if I tore it off."

"I—" She faltered, pulling away and biting her bottom lip. She tugged down the edge of the shirt, not looking at him. Her head shot up, and she brushed her lips over his.

Fuck professional boundaries. He twisted his fingers in her hair, tugging her head back and kissing her hard. She whimpered and pressed into him, body sliding against his. Every inch of him ached in response. He pushed until her back hit the door frame. His mouth worked down her neck, teeth nipping at the soft skin. God she tasted amazing. The soft flower of her perfume mingled with the faint salt of perspiration and made him lightheaded.

She pushed his shirt off his shoulders, and he let go of her long enough to let it drop. He rested one hand on the back of her neck, lips seeking hers out again, tongue dancing over hers. His other hand slid down her side, pushing the shirt out of the way until he met her bare waist. Her skin was soft against his palms.

Her nails raked over his undershirt, and he growled in response.

This was such a bad idea. He was hooked, and she would walk away in the morning, wearing her professional mask. He broke away abruptly.

She frowned, hurt reflected in her blue eyes.

But he would do anything to keep that look at bay, even if it destroyed him. Besides, there were worse ways to die a slow painful death than making love to the woman he was falling for. He grasped her wrists loosely in one hand and pushed her arms over her head, pinning her to the doorframe.

Her surprised gasp and follow-up moan seared his senses, obliterating any traces of thought about this being a bad idea. He pressed into her, holding her in place as he sucked along her neck. "Like this?" he asked, a growl vibrating through her skin.

She molded against him, frame soft and sensual, making him harder every time she shifted her weight. She whimpered and nodded.

He pressed his mouth to hers again, swallowing the intoxicating sounds of her reactions. Dropping his free hand to her waist, he pushed the shirt up again. She was hot against his palm as he slid it down her stomach. He wanted to be patient. To seduce her and prolong the moment. His lust disagreed; the desire to feel her, to taste her, to hear her cry out in pleasure sooner rather than later won out.

He dipped a hand under the elastic of her high-cut panties, seeking out her heat while his tongue danced around hers in a long kiss.

She ground against his hand when he found her already wet slit and glided down easily. Two fingers slid inside her, and she broke the kiss, her moan echoing through the condo. She shifted her weight, arms still trapped and limiting her movement. He smirked when she thrust against his hand, letting out a low growl when her hip pressed against his cock, rubbing through his slacks.

He brought his thumb to her clit, the swollen button eagerly greeting him, and she tilted her head back, eyes closed, lower lip caught between her teeth. Her breathing grew shallow as he pumped his fingers in and out, massaging her as she moved against him.

Her gasps came in short bursts, and her muscles gripped his fingers as she came. She shuddered and collapsed back against the wall, drawing away from his touch.

He wanted her badly and he wanted her now. He let go of her wrists, intending to lead her farther into the bedroom. Shock and a new wave of intense desire screamed through him when she pulled his hand from her waist instead. Hooded eyes never leaving his, she wrapped her tongue around his finger, drawing it into her mouth and slowly licking her juices from it.

He groaned with need. He couldn't take much more of the teasing, but he was loving every minute of the slow torture. She repeated the gesture again until she'd cleaned each of his fingers.

He reached for her, and she shook her head and stepped away. "Not this time."

He raised an eyebrow, the confidence making his cock throb harder.

She didn't say anything else as she trailed a fingernail down his chest, tracing along the waist of his slacks again. She reached the button and undid it, slowly pulling down his zipper.

A deep growl rumbled through his chest, anticipation making it difficult to think. She tugged his slacks and boxers down, and his arousal sprang free, cool air rushing in around it.

He swayed on his feet when she dropped to her knees. She drew her hands along his inner thighs. He watched in hungry anticipation as her tongue flicked out, brushing his bulbous head before she took him into her mouth.

He sucked in a fast breath through his teeth at the intense sensation, almost ready to burst from the simple touch. His knees went weak as her mouth slid down his shaft and he hit the back of her throat.

She stroked him as her tongue and lips glided along his length, the gesture slow at first, but increasing in pace in response to the guttural noises tearing from him. Her soft touch short-circuited his thoughts. The evaporating stress from the evening mingled with the hunger from her devouring him, and he felt himself drawing toward climax quickly.

"Kenz," he managed to gasp between pants. He tugged her arm, trying to pull her away.

She looked up at him, eyes wide and sparkling with mischief and determination. Her pace increased again, and she didn't pull away. Geez, that look. It was enough to push him over the edge. He wrapped his fingers in her hair, grunting as he came, still thrusting against her mouth as she swallowed him.

He shuddered as the last wave washed through him, and rested a hand against the wall to steady himself. She pulled away gently, licking him clean and sending another shudder through him at her soft tongue against his now hyper-sensitive skin.

He pulled her to her feet, fingers still tangled in her hair, and kissed her deeply. She sighed and pressed into him, nails digging into his back as she held him close. He gasped when they finally broke for air, lust still pumping through him.

He dropped his forehead against her shoulder. "You're still amazing." His words were marred by his heavy breathing. "Even more than last time I said it."

She trailed her nails up his spine, voice soft. "Only with you."

chapter fourteen

Kenzie snuggled into the sturdy body behind her, loving the feeling of Scott's arm wrapped around her. His blankets were soft and warm against her bare skin. She watched the sun creep across the floor through the heavy blinds, glinting off the glass of framed game artwork, industry awards. Glaring off photos on Scott's dresser of him with Zach and Rae. Warming the flannel sheets covering them both.

Ambivalence warred in her thoughts, making it difficult to completely enjoy the moment. The night before had been incredible, and she wanted it to happen again and again. Except that wasn't how purely physical relationships worked.

That and there was the tiny detail that she was sleeping with a client—something that could get her fired if anyone ever found out. Ever had a reason to question if it had been a conflict of interest.

A relationship she wanted more than almost anything, with a man she didn't think felt the same way. She was so screwed.

He kissed the back of her neck, breath warm on her skin, and pulled her closer. "Morning."

"Hey." Her voice was soft. She wanted to cling

to the perfectness of the morning as long as possible.

His hand moved up her thigh, stopping on her bare stomach. "I think I owe your sister a thank you note."

She smiled at the implication. "Don't encourage her. It doesn't always turn out this well."

He nipped at her shoulder. "I'm hoping it's never turned out this well. I'd hate to think I have competition."

She sighed at the light kisses, tilting her head back to give him access to her earlobe. A soft whimper slipped out when he accepted the invitation. "Speaking of family, you have so many pictures of yourself as an adult, where are the ones of you as a child?"

His posture shifted behind her, growing rigid for a moment before he relaxed. "I try and avoid my past. Daddy issues and all that."

Crap, she was ruining the moment. She didn't want that. "I'll file that under topics that make Scott McAllister uncomfortable, and we'll move on."

He pulled her closer, grip tightening around her for a moment in a squeeze before he relaxed again. "Nope, nothing makes me uncomfortable. But Scott Evans is still haunted by his childhood."

Had he really…? He had. His old last name. He'd just revealed a bit of the past she'd never been able to uncover. She should move on, change the subject, but she was curious. "Why does that name sound familiar?"

He exhaled. "You've probably seen the name on license plate rims."

Her eyes grew wide. Scott Evans owned a

massive chain of car dealerships across several states. "So you're … really?"

"Yeah, he's my father."

Wow. The shock sank in. It didn't change how she felt about him, but there was something about knowing he'd come from so much money that boggled her mind. He was so down to earth.

He molded against her again, but something felt off. His lips slid along her shoulder. "Not that I mind talking about my past, except that I kind of do, so instead can I buy you breakfast?"

In public. On a weekend. With a client and very obviously wearing his clothes. This time she was the one to stiffen. She failed to keep the discomfort to herself. "Do you get room service up here?"

He dropped his arm and sat, pushing away from her. "I meant the diner on the corner. They make an incredible omelet. Unless French toast is more your thing."

Her brow furrowed. She needed to save this. Get the warmth and comfort back. She rolled onto her back and tilted her head up enough to brush her lips over his, propping herself up on her elbows. "I'm enjoying the moment. I bet we could figure out something to do here."

He didn't return the kiss, jaw set in a hard line. "Please don't do this."

She stuck out her lower lip. "Do what? The company is nice. It should be like this more often."

He stood and backed away. "Hidden from public view like the uncle no one mentions at Thanksgiving because he's in prison?"

She slumped back, arms crossed over her chest.

"Don't be like this."

"Right, this is all on me." He shook his head and turned away. "I'll call you a cab to take you back to your car." He riffled through his drawer and pulled out a pair of sweats. "Sorry I don't have anything less *me* to loan you. If you take the back elevator, no one will notice you leaving."

The ice in his voice devoured her almost as much as his implication, but she couldn't take it back. She was right about needing to stay discreet.

Kenzie stepped from the elevator, the sight of the all-glass office making her gut do another somersault. She didn't know if she should be here, but the meeting was already on her calendar, and since he hadn't canceled, she wasn't going to pass up the opportunity to see him again. Not that she knew what she would say. She wanted him so much, and she so very much couldn't have him.

She steeled her resolve and tried to push her emotions aside. She needed to be removed. It was the only option since they were still working together.

She pasted a smile in place as she approached the receptionist. The girl looked up, joy genuine. "Scott says you can go on back."

"Thanks." Kenzie kept walking, afraid if she paused to make small talk she wouldn't be able to make her feet move again. She could do this. She was in control; she could make it through this meeting. They were just touching base, and she'd never seen Scott stay angry, so she was probably stressed about nothing.

He glanced up when she paused in the doorway and then nodded to the chair across from his desk. "I'm sorry, I need to finish this email. I'll be right with you, Miss Carter."

She winced at the formality. But it was necessary, right? She let the door swing shut behind her.

He still didn't look at her. "You sure you don't want that open? People might talk."

Ouch. She took her seat. "I'm sure it will be fine." She crossed her legs and folded her hands on her knees, eyes growing wide when she took a second glance at him. He was wearing a black button-down and a pencil tie that made his stern expression almost malevolent. He looked gorgeous. And so very not himself.

He finally turned his attention to her. "I'm sorry again to keep you waiting. Did we have an agenda?" There was no catch in his voice. No sarcasm or bitterness. Or anything.

It was exactly what it should be. So why did it make her skin crawl? She pulled a printout from her bag and slid it across the desk. "I'm sorry I didn't make copies, but I know what's on there."

He scanned the print out. "It's my schedule for the next few weeks."

"That's right. That's the agenda." She stopped herself at the last minute, deciding not to put emphasis on the word "agenda." "You've got a charity function in a few days. I wanted to make sure you have everything you need."

His expression stayed flat. "I'm not sure. The invite says casual, but I don't know if that means khakis and an Izod, or Oxford and a tie."

She furrowed her brow. "It probably means casual."

"I don't think so." He shook his head. "*Cosmo* says business men in jeans are the leading cause of global warming."

Seriously? She couldn't take it anymore. "Why are you acting like this?"

He looked at her, dark eyes blank. "I don't understand."

She clenched her teeth. "This formal bullshit. What are you doing?"

His smile looked painted on. "It may have escaped your attention, but your contract cost us a lot of money. I'm trying to get some use out of it. Isn't this what you wanted?"

Something throbbed in her chest. "I didn't want you to completely surrender yourself."

His smile vanished, the eerie flat expression returning to take its place. He stood, hands clasped, and moved to stand behind her chair. "You're sure?"

She wouldn't give him the satisfaction of turning. "I'm positive. This isn't about being someone else. It's all about appearances."

"Of course." He traced a finger up the back of her bare neck. "Appearances are important." His voice was low and smooth. "So help me out because I think I'm still missing something." His fingertips glided along her collarbone. "I'm not allowed to flirt where someone might see." He trailed up her jaw. "But behind closed doors you can do whatever you want." His breath brushed the outside of her ear. "And then you throw a fit when I finally act the way you tell me to."

The cold in his voice was a shocking contrast to his warm touch. She desperately wanted to sink into the gesture, but forced herself to stay upright. Air rushed in around her when his hand dropped away. She could tell he had stepped back, but didn't know how far and wasn't going to cave and look.

"So we need some ground rules." His voice was low, seductive. "I can have you when you're in the mood? You can tease me as long as I don't take it too seriously? If I let anyone get to know the real me, my entire livelihood is destroyed?"

Every word bit deeper, but she didn't know what else to do. It was also all true, at least as long as they were working together. She was on her feet in an instant, spinning to face him. Her breath caught when she realized how close he was standing. Her heels kept her at eye level with him, and his gaze threatened to capture her.

She pushed it all aside. "This isn't easy for me either. I want you desperately." The confession slipped out before she could stop it. Screw it, no one was looking, she could be honest. "Walking that fine line between how attracted I am to you and how damaging indulging would be to my career is devastating." She hesitated and then brushed her lips over his.

Her pulse screamed in anticipation when he tangled his fingers in her hair and pulled her head back. His lips brushed her throat, and she gasped in response.

"So I can have you right now?" His hungry growl rolled through the room. "While no one is watching?"

She wanted to be bold, aggressive, in control. But she wanted him more. "Yes."

He let go and stepped away until the door stopped him. He clasped his hands behind his back, gaze never leaving her. "So you can keep your job and still get what you want? So you don't have to tell anyone the scruffy-looking nerfherder with the massive ego made you scream in pleasure just by talking to you?"

His eyes never left hers, and she realized it was hurt staring back at her, not the barely controlled fury she expected. His voice was quiet, but firm. "I'm not here to sate whatever repressed bad-girl desires you've built up. I'm not the guy you call because you want to get off, and no one else is naughty enough. Fuck, if that's what you're looking for, I am so very tame. Or maybe you're not ready for more than that yet. As long as I don't get any kinkier, you can still claim you're a good girl?"

It ripped through her to hear her own motivations thrown back in her face. Tore at her to hear it laid out so coldly and to realize how much it was hurting him.

He looked away finally. "Fuck it. I'm tired of trying to guess what's going on in your head. You want me, you don't want to be around me, I irritate you, I excite you, and God forbid anyone knows how desperately I want to fuck you. Or even worse, that it might run deeper than that."

She closed the distance between them, staring him down and hating herself for what she had to say. "I don't know what you want from me. This was never meant to be serious. It was a kiss in a parking lot between strangers. A flirt in a dressing room to take off the edge. A couple of naughty words in the heat of the moment. It's become counterproductive."

His smile was cold. "You're really fond of that phrase, aren't you Miss Carter? Contrary to what you think, I'm not incompetent. I'm not an idiot. I've survived the last decade without your help, and you don't want to be here, so tell me, why are you? What keeps you coming back?"

She couldn't answer that question. She'd asked herself the same thing a million times, and her gut always clenched when she got close to an answer. Screw this. "That's it, we're done," she snarled. "Move."

"Answer my question."

She glared at him, forcing the lie out and hating the way it burned past her lips and left a gaping void inside. "Nothing. There is nothing to keep me coming back."

His mask slipped, hurt and disbelief rushing in to replace it, and he stepped aside, opening the door as he moved. "Got it."

chapter fifteen

Scott drummed his fingers against his keyboard, clacking against the keys and spewing random letters across his code. He should clean that up. Not that it mattered. He hadn't written anything usable since Kenzie had left anyway.

He was still furious about the way she'd stormed out, but worse, he was upset at himself for letting it happen. He'd slipped one too many times with her. He'd tipped his hand and at the same time forced hers. As much as he wished she felt even half for him what he felt for her, she still saw a distinct line between their physical and professional relationships.

He closed his eyes and inhaled deeply. What would it take to get her back? He'd stop everything, the fooling around, the flirting, all of it, if he could at least apologize to her. Maybe get her to stay on and finish her contract.

He grabbed his desk phone, dialing her number from memory. It rang once, twice. He sighed. Please let her answer.

"This is Mackenzie." Her tone sent ice over the line.

He slid into his business-meeting voice. "Miss Carter. Good afternoon."

Her exhale was loud against the receiver. "I've had better. What can I do for you?"

He flinched at her removed response. Would she even listen if he begged for forgiveness? "I think we parted ways on a bad note."

"What gave you that impression?"

He hated what he was about to do, but at least knowing she didn't hate him would be something, even if he couldn't actually have more. "That was my fault. I haven't been fair to you."

Silence.

He let a bitter smile show for his invisible audience. "I'd like to set things right. Have lunch with me tomorrow."

More silence.

He could wait longer.

"I assume your associates will be there?" she asked.

He glared at the phone. "I hadn't planned on it."

Her reply was devoid of emotion. "You're not that sorry if you're still peddling this fake dating crap."

He swallowed the slash her words cut through him. "Of course, my mistake. Yes, all of our consultants are invited."

He intentionally neglected to mention Rae was the only other one they kept on payroll, and she was so buried in end-of-month reporting, she'd beg off something frivolous like lunch.

More silence.

He kept his mouth shut.

"Sounds great." Her tone implied it sounded anything but. "Email me a meeting request, I'll try and make room in my schedule."

"Wonderful. Enjoy the rest of your day, Miss Carter."

He hated that the situation required such an intense formality. But he was willing to keep doing it if it meant she'd be around long enough so he could figure out how to not need it. Something in his chest fluttered that she'd said yes, and somehow that made it better.

♥♥♥

Nervous energy thrummed through Kenzie as she approached the restaurant. The parking lot was packed, but experience told her it wouldn't matter— they wouldn't have to wait. And the reason why was on the sidewalk pacing near the front door.

Scott looked up as she approached, a smile twitching into place and then vanishing again in an instant.

She cursed the leap in her stomach, hiding the happy reaction behind a flat expression, and nodded at him.

"We have a problem." His voice didn't give anything away.

"We have a lot of them." She hid her wince. She hadn't meant to be antagonistic.

He raised an eyebrow. "Nice. I mean my timing was bad. Everyone else cancelled."

Go figure. She wasn't surprised or nearly as irritated as she wanted to be. In fact, if she weren't ignoring it, she might have admitted she'd hoped and expected exactly that. "Everyone else. Rae?" He flinched. "How convenient."

He shrugged. "I'm sorry to drag you all the way out here for nothing. I should let you get back to your pliable clients. It wouldn't do for us to be unchaperoned. What would people say?"

Why was she even letting him get away with this? It had nothing to do with how good he looked in the navy button-down and dark jeans, or the snippets of memory taunting her from the weekend, of waking up in his arms. Or because despite the professional risk, she so desperately wanted an intimacy from him that went beyond sex. "We're here, we might as well stay. I'm sure you can behave yourself in public just this once."

He gave her a wilting smile. "I might find a way."

Why did they have to do this? When had they become incapable of having a normal conversation that didn't end in frustration?

He refused to make eye contact when they were seated, but was happy to talk to everyone else, including a lengthy discussion about the special with the waitress.

Then they were alone again. Scott traced the patterns on the table.

"So." Kenzie didn't like the silence. She could make small talk, right? Something simple. Non-inflammatory. "It's too bad Rae couldn't make it. The two of you have this synergy that's fascinating to watch." She felt a twinge of jealousy toward the other woman simply because Rae and Scott never had to hide their interactions. What would it be like to be open about how she felt about him? How she didn't dare hope he felt about her?

The corner of his mouth twitched, but he didn't look at her. "I'm glad I could entertain you. Synergy. Did you pull that from a buzzword thesaurus?"

"You know what I mean. You just click."

He finally glanced up. "We grew up together. She and Zach are pretty much the reason I survived adolescence."

That genuine joy was back in his face when he talked about it. The smile, the gleam in his eye. She so rarely saw that when… She bit back a sigh. When she was the focus of the conversation. "That must be nice."

He studied her for a minute. "You've got something similar with Riley, right?"

She shook her head. "Riley is a selfish pest."

He winked at her. "So the two of you have that in common."

She twisted her mouth in irritation. "Thanks."

"You know I'm teasing." He reached over the table, brushed his thumb over her knuckles, and pulled back abruptly as if he'd been shocked. "Sorry."

She wanted to tell him it wasn't a big deal, but it was. "The thing about Riley is she's always telling me I have to loosen up. That I'm too uptight, I need to unwind, stuff like that."

He raised an eyebrow. "Gee, it must be tough having someone dictate how you should act. I can't imagine."

She took a sip of her water. "It's different with you. You're my job."

"So you keep saying."

This wasn't going well. "About the other night." She fingered the pendant at the base of her throat. "Or rather, the other morning. I should have been more diplomatic."

His brow creased. "Is that difficult?"

"What?" She didn't know what he was talking about.

"Apologizing without actually accepting responsibility?"

The words stung, but she knew she deserved it. She gave a sad smile. "As long I don't have to admit I was wrong."

His chuckle sounded forced and ended in a sigh. "So, we have to scale this back to completely professional."

"Yes."

"No more sex, seduction, secret meetings."

It was harder to force out her "Exactly" than she expected. "But we can still stay friends."

"Are we really?"

She looked at him, unable to ignore the combination of hurt and question in his eyes. "Friends? Of course."

"So, if I randomly called you for a cup of coffee, you'd say yes?"

Why did she feel like this was a setup? But there was nothing deceptive in his face. "Of course. As long as I was available."

His smile was weak. "Of course."

This was devouring her. She just wanted to dive into his arms. To bury her head in his chest. To pretend everything was all right between them. Her heart thudded, and she frowned. "I'm so sorry. I wish it didn't have to be this way."

"Me too." He fiddled with his fork. "So this charity dinner, you're coming right?"

She hadn't expected the rapid shift in topic. "I hadn't planned on it."

The corner of his mouth pulled up in that half smile that so frequently disarmed her. "You have to come. It's a massive industry affair, it's for an amazing cause, and the theme this year is masquerade."

And that joy was back in his eyes that didn't show through very often. That enthusiasm that always made her want to know more. This time it also increased her guilt. She'd never investigated the dinner since it was private and casual, and she figured she'd have more luck asking him to behave in his own living room. "I shouldn't admit this, but I don't know what it's for."

He leaned in, intertwined fingers resting on the table. "It's this auction, right? Everyone in the industry donates rare and one-of-a-kind items, someone donates the catering and the building, and every single cent, from the door price to the money raised, goes to schools with low budgets so they can give their kids access to technology and more basic things like books and supplies."

"Oh." The entire concept made his smile infectious. "I could be on board for that. But masquerade? I don't even dress up for Halloween."

"Of course you don't." There was no accusation in his voice. "This is easy though. You just have to come as your favorite game character."

"Uh…" That was going to be a problem. "So first of all, I don't really game, you know that, so I don't have a favorite anything. And second, most female game characters don't wear a lot of clothing."

He didn't look deterred. "If you know that much, you can figure out the rest. And it's true. About half the women there will be wearing the equivalent of a swimsuit, and the other half will find an alternative or pick male characters. Then again, the same could be said about the men. Expect to see your share of hairy chests in chainmail bikinis."

She twisted her mouth, hoping to hide her amusement behind disgust. "I don't even want to picture that."

"You don't have to." He winked. "Say you'll be there, and you can live it for yourself. I promise it's not a date or anything." He added quickly. "I just…"

She studied him when he didn't finish the thought. This type of uncertainty was so rare for him. "Yes?"

He didn't look at her. "Come see that I'm not the asshole screw-up you think I am and enjoy a fantastic night for a good cause at the same time."

The doubt and self-effacing ate at her. "I don't think you're an asshole screw-up."

He looked at her, one eyebrow raised, mouth twisted in disbelief. "Yeah, okay."

Those two words gnawed at something inside. She pushed her lunch away, suddenly not hungry. It completely devoured her that the rift between them seemed irreparable.

chapter sixteen

Scott laughed along with Jared Tippins—an old friend, and head of development for one of the top cyber security firms in the country.

Scott tried to focus on the conversation, but his attention kept drifting to the door. He should have known Kenzie wouldn't come. They weren't exactly on the best terms, and her insistence they were still friends had been weak.

Still, he'd hoped she might buy in for such a great cause. Or for work.

He adjusted his battle dress uniform and fingered the fake scar on his face. At least his Solid Snake costume was drawing positive attention.

"I didn't think you could top that new-in-box N64 from last year," Jared said. "Where the fuck did you dig up an Atari 2600?"

Scott shrugged. "I know a girl who knows a guy."

"Yeah, yeah. If I had your contact list…" Jared didn't really do the whole *costume* thing—he'd probably get along great with Kenzie. This year he wore a plastic guitar-shaped controller, said he was a *Guitar Hero* extra.

"Well, if I had your security knowledge."

Jared smirked. "Trade you."

"No you wouldn't." This part of the conversation rarely changed between them. Besides, Scott's list wasn't for sale, Jared's skill was. Hell, they taught some of Jared's network security theories in colleges.

A random Laura Croft nudged Jared. "You any good with that thing?"

Scott chuckled. She might be joking, but she'd asked the wrong guy that question. Or the right one.

"I'm decent." Jared swung the toy guitar into place like he was going to play it, and proceeded to belt out the first chorus of an incredible acapella version of *I Want You to Want Me*.

A smattering of applause erupted around them, but it faded into a murmur that ran through the room.

Scott snagged snippets of "no way" and "hot", and turned his attention to the door.

The woman near the entrance was tall. In the four-inch stilettos she was probably a hint taller than him. The back latex covering her skin and matching face paint obstructed who she was. But the way the black miniskirt hugged her waist, the wide gold belt, the gold bikini top, the blonde hair falling around her shoulders and down her back … Scott knew exactly who it was.

Unless she'd sent her twin in her place, but he doubted that.

"Drow's not a video game character," a man nearby complained.

"Invitation said game character," a woman corrected him. "Besides, she's hot. I'm not complaining."

Scott bit back a smile, eyes meeting Kenzie's across the room. Her expression remained flat, and she made a straight line to him, not pausing for anyone.

Scott still couldn't take his eyes off her. *Wow.* She'd showed. And please let her leave alone if it wasn't with him. She stopped next to them, nodding at his colleagues. "Males." Her voice rang heavy with disdain. "Fellow warrior." She nodded at the head programmer, a woman from a competing company.

And she was in character too. Scott resisted the urge to play along and drop to one knee, asking how he could please his queen.

She looked at him again, expression cold. "You will speak with me now."

A round of snickers erupted around him. He didn't care. "Yes, ma'am."

"Lucky bastard," someone else muttered as they walked away.

He followed her toward an emptier corner of the room, gaze traveling up her bare back—well, latex-covered—struggling not to close the distance between them. Half the eyes in the room were on them, and she'd definitely smack him for real. They ducked out through a side door, but the cool night air on his face didn't push away the heat in his veins.

His voice was heavy, but he managed to keep the teasing hint present. "So, am I supposed to kiss your boots, my queen? Because I'm fully prepared to do so."

She finally faced him again, panic heavy in her

blue eyes and stern expression gone. "Oh, gawd, I can't believe I let Riley talk me into this. Everyone in there was staring. I should have worn something else. Something less … let-my-assets-hang-out."

"Whoa." He forced his hand to stay by his side, worried if he reached for her he wouldn't be able to stop. "You look amazing, you're wearing more than half the people in there, and you're blending. I swear."

She scowled. "I saw Hank Cartee in there. You didn't tell me he was going to be here."

He gave her what he hoped was an apologetic smile. "I didn't think about it. Consider this your warning, he'll be at pretty much anything that's industry-wide."

Her brow creased, adding a new layer of haunting to the regal costume. "How many more of these do you think I'll be attending?"

Her implication that she either didn't want to be there or didn't want to be spending time with him—he wasn't sure which—stung, and he tried to hide it. "As many as I can get away with. I like having you here, and I'll keep you on retainer if that's what it takes."

She put more space between them, mouth twisted in irritation. "I'm not Julia Roberts. My job isn't to attend fancy parties with you."

Shit, she'd taken the compliment wrong.

"I know, and I didn't mean to imply. You're not, it's true. You're far more attractive, and I suspect infinitely more intelligent. Also, if we're making *Pretty Woman* references, I'm Julia Roberts, and you're grooming me so no one knows I'm a whore."

He grinned big.

She let out a small laugh, and her entire frame relaxed. "You'd never pull off that mini with suspenders."

"I might could, you never know." He wanted to lean in and kiss the concern away. Ease the stress from around her lips. He stepped closer.

"Miss Carter." Hank Cartee's voice cut through the night. "I didn't expect to see you here."

Scott stepped back instead. Kenzie's back went straight, and her impassive mask slammed back into place. "It's for a good cause. I have to keep an eye on my male." She nodded at Scott, her posture, tone, and language indicating she was role playing again as the dominant character she'd dressed as.

Hank didn't even glance in Scott's direction, eyes locked on her chest. He finally looked at her face. "Of course. And you do know how to make an entrance. Listen, I'll let you two get back to discussing business soon—though don't do it too much, this is a party, right?" He laughed, though no one else did.

Scott's hands clenched into fists, but he kept them hidden behind his back, not having a reason to interrupt.

"Anyway." Hank took Kenzie's fingers between his, and kissed her knuckles. "You look amazing, my dear, and I had to come out here and let you know, and also apologize for how I acted when we met. It was inappropriate. I know you must be incredible at what you do to have made this kind of impact, and I never should have implied otherwise."

Kenzie's stern expression wavered, and she

pulled her hand away. "Of course. Water under the bridge, Mr. Cartee. Now if you'll excuse me, I have to get back inside."

Hank held the door open for her, still never looking directly at Scott, and let it swing shut behind them.

Scott stood in the night air for several minutes after they were gone, breathing deep and trying to remember not to hyperventilate. He pushed back his fury at Cartee and the very visible reaction he'd had to Kenzie. Great, he was a kid again who couldn't even control a hard-on. Fantastic.

Kenzie stood near the back of the room, shifting her weight from one foot to another. Standing up straight made her heels ache, but fidgeting didn't solve the problem. She desperately wanted to step out of the torture devices masquerading as shoes. She sipped her water and watched as item after item sold to the highest bidder.

It made her smile that so many people were into the evening. Or at least, now that the novelty of snapping pictures of everyone in their costumes had worn off and she had some peace, it made her smile.

She'd mingled a little, but this wasn't the kind of affair she was used to. Scott was in his element. Every time she caught a glimpse of him, he was laughing and joking with someone new. She didn't know which were his colleagues and which were just fans, but he seemed to enjoy everyone's company. Such a sharp contrast to how drained he'd looked at the investor dinner.

Could she sneak out for the night without saying goodbye? Was it rude to leave before the auction was over? She set her drink on a nearby table and made her way toward the exit, relieved when she didn't pass anyone. The lights and noise faded into the background, and she left it behind her with a hint of regret.

A warm hand landed at the small of her back, startling her and obliterating her musings, and a faint whiff of cologne greeted her. It was him. She stopped in the empty, quiet hallway. At least he couldn't hear her hammering heart.

His breath was warm on her neck, his voice low. "What they're saying is true. You really are the most beautiful woman here."

The compliment warmed her, and she couldn't fight the flutter that surged through her chest. She tried to push it away, stay aloof, and hope it didn't show on the surface. "Really? How many of the others have you said that to?"

"Not a single one." Hurt was distinct in his reply.

She winced at the wounded honesty, but hid her reaction, never turning to face him.

"It's a shame we're just associates. Friends at best." He moved closer until his entire left side was pressed against her back, hand on her hip and finger tracing a light line along the top of her skirt. "Because I desperately want to take you home with me."

Her skin flushed from the contact and the sincere words, and she was glad the makeup and latex hid it. She spun, any response dying on her lips when she met his gaze. She traced a finger over his face beneath the fake scar. "This is sexy, but I'm glad it's not real."

He inhaled through clenched teeth, a reluctant smile flitting in. "Me too. Getting something like this probably hurts like hell."

She laughed and ducked her head. It was too easy. Too much fun.

He stepped closer, and she locked her gaze on him again, sinking into the deep brown of his eyes. He traced a finger over her bottom lip, and an electrified chill ran through her. Her lips parted, and her eyes half drifted shut as she leaned in.

His mouth found hers, and her heart hammered in response to the gentle kiss. He deepened the gesture, hand moving to the small of her back and holding her close. She pressed tightly against him, memorizing every inch of how his body felt against hers, his distinct reaction digging into her hip.

A loud giggle echoed through the empty hallway, sounding like shattering glass in the otherwise still.

Her eyes flew open, and she broke the kiss as she remembered how very public their surroundings were. She forced one foot back, and then the other, putting a several inches between them. Her laugh sounded forced and nervous, even to her own ears, and disappointment warred with propriety. "This might not be the time."

He studied her for a moment, expression finally breaking into a sad smile. "Had to give it a shot, right?" Hurt rang heavy in his fake laughter. "Anyway, I'm out of here soon, just wanted to tell you good night. Thank you for coming."

He kept the distance between them, and her disappointment grew.

"See you." He moved away, not shaking her hand, or kissing her cheek, or anything, before he faded back into the crowd.

She slumped against a nearby wall, beating back the desire to chase him down. To tell him it didn't matter. To admit how very much she wanted to leave with him too. Too bad that wouldn't be appropriate.

chapter seventeen

Kenzie pushed her laptop out of the way, resting her arms on her desk and her chin on her arms. She didn't know why she was trying to work. She hadn't gotten any done for the last two days.

Her bedroom wall stared back at her, the off-white texture not giving her any answers. Every time she tried to do something, anything, even basic things like sleeping, thoughts of Scott haunted her. His arm wrapped around her while she drifted off. Waking up with his chest pressed against her back. His finger on her lips before he faded back into the crowds at the masquerade.

The wounded pain in his eyes. How very much she just needed to walk away but couldn't.

Something tickled her thoughts, but she couldn't place it. It nudged and nagged until she grabbed it. A way out, maybe?

Things were going well, right? No public incidents, Cartee had said himself at the charity auction that things were better. So that meant she was probably almost done. She could transfer the contract to someone new, say it was in maintenance mode. Or cancel it altogether. If the issue was resolved, there was no reason for her to stay on, right? He'd proved he could clean up when the situation called for it. He knew how to behave. He was absolutely charming when he wanted to be.

He was everything perfect. And if she could just get out of that damn contract, maybe they had a chance together. If he was even still interested in her.

It was the most soothing thought she'd had since they parted ways after the auction. She smiled and turned her head, resting her cheek on her arms and letting the possibilities flit through her thoughts. They would be incredible together at formal parties. He had looked amazing in that tux. The thought tugged something unpleasant, but she pushed away the nagging. More clothes shopping. That had been fun.

The nagging grew, but she couldn't tell what it was attached to.

Her computer chimed, and she forced the fantasy away.

A message from Zach.

We need to talk. I'd expect this from Scott, but not you.

Nausea slipped through her, and her temple throbbed. What the hell? She was reaching for her phone when her email chimed again. This time it was a message from Greta.

I need you in my office this afternoon. Tell me when you're available, I'll make time.

A link to a gaming forum followed the message. She clicked through, curiosity mingling with unfocused dread as the page loaded. Her eyes grew wide at what she saw, and her stomach lurched. Oh shit. What had they done?

The forum thread was titled: *Why I rly wnt 2 b a game designer.*

And it was full of photos from the charity dinner. The amazing costumes, the fantastic fun. The black-skinned drow she'd dressed as tucked in a dark hallway, Scott's finger on her lip, the two of them looking very much just seconds from kissing. Then another shot of their lips pressed together, his hand on her lower back, her palms resting on his chest.

Enough evidence that she'd been intimate with a client to jeopardize her job. A mile-long string of profanities raced through her thoughts. How had that gotten on camera? Damn it, why had she let herself fall into this?

Panic pounded through her, overriding reason as she dove into reactionary mode. She had to fix this. She couldn't let it impact her job.

She tried to call Zach, but went straight to voicemail. She hung up before the beep, not sure what to say. She replied to Greta, saying she'd be there in half an hour.

She forwarded the message with links to Scott and included her own message.

Never again.

She scurried to dress and pull her hair back so she could get into the office. Her email chimed again with a reply from Scott.

Fine with me.

She snarled at her laptop and slammed it shut. Fury and hurt screamed through her veins. The finality in those three words. Her stomach rolled in on itself as she walked out the door. He didn't get to have the last word in this. She slipped in her earpiece and dialed his number as she headed to her car. Her heels scuffed against the concrete. She didn't care.

"What?" His gruff voice greeted her.

"That's my question." She slid into her car, letting every bit of her frustration pour into her voice. "What the hell is wrong with you?"

"Really?" Anger and disbelief poured through the receiver. "You called to bitch me out, instead of, oh, I don't know, admitting this was a shared moment? Or if I really mean that little to you, doing damage control?"

"Damage control." She spit the phrase out in disgust. She pulled onto the road, maneuvering through traffic. "I don't have an emergency contingency plan for you being a careless fuckup. Just because you never wanted to do this publicity thing doesn't give you the right to waste my time and your company's money. You may have gotten me fired. Do you even care?"

"Do I even care?" His laugh was short and harsh. "What a funny thing for you to ask. So this is still all about business? About your career?" His snide tone assaulted her ears.

There was something hidden in the question, there always was with him, but she couldn't figure out what. "And yours."

"You're lying. And you're so far removed from the professional you're pretending to be right now, it's not even funny."

She gritted her teeth at the accusation, hissing inwardly at the part of her that asked if he had a point. "How dare you? You arrogant, presumptuous asshole.”

“Right, of course. This is all on me.” His tone slid into that mocking calm that meant he was backing down because he thought she was being stubborn, not because he knew she was right. “Zach wants to talk to you. And me. I assume that means we won’t have to work together anymore. That should come as a relief to you.”

“Damn straight.”

“I’d say it was nice working with you, Miss Carter.” Fake charm dripped from his voice. “But I’d be lying. Goodbye.”

The line clicked dead before she could respond, but fortunately also before her sob slipped out. She gripped the steering wheel until her fingers ached. She maneuvered to the side of the road and turned on her emergency lights, putting the car in park. The leather was hot against her forehead as she leaned into it. She breathed deep, struggling to calm down. His parting words echoed in her head, threatening to evict her breakfast, and unshed tears stung her eyes. What had just happened?

Anger, hurt, betrayal. Scott didn’t know which emotion he wanted to focus on. Whichever made him the most miserable and distracted him from the distinct ache in his chest. The conversation echoed in his head, mocking him, throbbing against his skull. He slammed his fist into his couch, letting the padding absorb the impact, and disappointed it hadn’t hurt more. At least then he’d have a focus for his … everything.

He couldn't do this anymore. He didn't know when he'd started falling for her, but it was agonizingly obvious it didn't work both ways. It was time to stop pretending otherwise. He grabbed his phone.

"The board is not happy with you," Zach greeted him before the first ring finished.

Fuck the board. He rolled his eyes. "You mean Cartee isn't happy with me. I have a solution, I want her gone."

"That will work splendidly with the people wondering if you hired her because you were sleeping with her."

Scott snarled, anger and frustration spilling from him. "I wanted to send her packing the first day she showed up in the office. You hired her."

Zach sighed. "Not that it matters, but you're right. Still, firing her doesn't fix anything."

"Neither does keeping her on. Neither did hiring her." Scott hated it when they hit a wall. He could plow through almost anyone's bullshit, but talking over Zach took a talent he didn't know if he had the patience for right now. "I don't even care. Tell them it was my fault, that you're picking the next one, whatever."

"Cartee isn't the only one who's upset."

Those words sent a chill through Scott. He had to force himself to ask for details. "Oh?"

"All you had to do was play along. Pretend you'd taken this edict seriously." Zach's tone was weary. "It was so simple. And now instead, you've spit in the board's face—shown them you think you're above their requests, that you're so arrogant that you can fuck around instead of complying with a simple request—and they're considering Cartee's call for a vote to fire you."

Scott flopped back against the couch, head hitting the cushion hard and stars dancing in front of his eyes, blurring his view of the ceiling. "Shit."

"Meet me somewhere." Zach's sigh filled the line, and in the background the click of a lighter bled through. "We need to talk about this face to face."

Was it actually that serious? No. Scott was so done playing nice. Bowing to people. Surrendering everything he believed in just for someone to try and steal his company at the end of the day. "I have work to do."

"Scott."

"Zach." He spit his best friend's name back, tired of the conversation. "Fire her. Bring someone else on if it floats your boat. I have contracts to read."

He disconnected before he could get any argument. He was done with Kenzie. She didn't want him around and he was fine with that. Or maybe he would be if the gaping hole in his chest ever mended.

But in the meantime, he knew there were failsafe's built into every board member's agreement to keep things like this from happening. He might not be able to save his personal life, but he could sure as hell try and find a way to evict Cartee from his professional one.

He pushed aside the gnawing ache in his chest pleading with him to call her, to make it right. She didn't want him in her bed or anywhere in her life. He didn't care. Not at all. Not one single little bit.

He draped his arm over his forehead, blocking

out the world. *Fuck.*

He pushed himself up, staring at his laptop, the forum images taunting him of the shared moment—probably the last time he'd get to kiss that amazing woman. The realization devoured him.

Something caught his eye, and he took a closer look. The photo had crappy resolution, like it had been taken from a distance. A phone probably, which didn't surprise him. But that wasn't what mattered. It was the user name on the post.

A screen name he'd seen dozens of times during beta tests. One of the perks of being a board member was Cartee's kid always got a first look at what they were putting out.

Hank's son had posted the photos. Scott snarled and punched the couch again. That son of a bitch had set him up.

Too bad he didn't know what to do with the information. He sank back into the cushions again, fury, hurt, and resignation flooding him and making his limbs heavy.

His phone buzzed at his side. He didn't want to talk to anyone else. Still, he grabbed it, irritation swelling inside when he saw who it was. It would probably serve him to ignore the call, but this was one person he didn't mind taking his frustration out on.

His tone was flat when he answered. "It's not my birthday or Christmas, what's the occasion?"

A smooth, confident voice replied, "I just wanted to talk to my son. Is that a crime?"

"I don't know, Dad. Is it?" On second thought, this had been a bad idea. His father never called him out of the blue. Why today? Of all the days in the entirety of his adult life, why now?

"It's nice to hear from you too." There was no sarcasm in the older man's voice. It was implied in the flat response. "But since you're insisting there must be something wrong, I heard you were having some business problems."

Scott's eyes narrowed, a sick feeling swimming through him. Something wasn't right. The entire day wasn't right, but this was just completely out there. "Where did you hear that?"

"Brokers, traders. Whispers are starting to run through Wall Street."

Scott clenched his jaw. He was being lied to. "We're not publicly traded. Wall Street doesn't give a rat's ass about us."

A loud sigh echoed through the receiver. "All right. I had lunch with an old friend, Hank Cartee. Apparently you two do business together?"

Scott choked back his disbelief. "What?"

"He mentioned things aren't going your way right now."

Scott stared at the forum name in front of him, too many thoughts swirling in his head to make sense of them.

"I'm not surprised you're in trouble." His father's voice was distant, but as condescending as ever. "You've gotten in over your head this time. It would be in your best interest to have someone else step in and take the reins."

A growl slipped out, and Scott didn't try and hide it. Rage screamed through him. "Thanks. I'm fine." He disconnected and threw his phone aside. He grabbed his laptop, fingers flying over the keyboard as he dug deeper into Hank's past than he ever had before. He followed thread after thread of where his money came from, who he knew, and who he associated with.

His phone buzzed again, and he shut it off without looking. This was going to take a while, and he didn't need any more interruptions.

Kenzie sat in the chair outside Greta's office, toes tapping inside her shoes, fingers drumming on her knees. A gaping ache throbbed in her chest, and she hadn't been able to make it go away, regardless of how hard she tried to push Scott's words from her mind.

It didn't matter. She still had a job to do, and that included damage control. As much for herself as anyone. She'd spin the pictures as harmless—part of being in character, of fitting in at the charity auction. She could get the word out right, and people would know she was professional enough she hadn't crossed that line.

Her chest ached in response to the thought, and she took a deep breath.

"Come on in." Greta stood in the doorway, nodding into the office.

Kenzie pasted her most professional smile in place and took a seat across from the other woman's desk. Her gut sank further at the sound of a latching door behind her. It needed to be a private meeting, she knew that, but it still made her nervous.

"I've got an entire plan to correct this." The

words tumbled past Kenzie's lips the moment Greta was seated. "It's based largely on the emergency contingency we outlined. I'll get counter posts out immediately, explanations, I can have a formal proposal in front of you in sixty minutes, and—"

Greta held up a hand, cutting her off. "I have someone else working on that already based on the plans you've laid out in the past. We have more important things to discuss."

"Someone else is working my contract?" Kenzie frowned. It was what she'd wanted just a couple of hours ago, but she'd wanted it on her terms. This wasn't right.

Greta wouldn't meet her gaze, attention focused on her computer instead. "The client requested you be removed. Not that we could have let you stay on given the situation. We've also pulled you out of the rotation for any new jobs."

Rinslet had already fired her? Kenzie's stomach threatened to revolt. And she was being suspended. That wasn't fair. She hadn't even been given a chance to make it right. "Can I ask why?"

Greta glanced at her, eyebrow raised. "Really? This isn't about the client's image, it's about ours. We don't cross that line. I thought you of all people understood that. You were even warned."

"I didn't—" The denial froze in her throat; she couldn't make herself say it. She couldn't force out the insistence that it wasn't what it looked like. "I can fix it. Just give me a chance." She heard and hated the pleading in her own voice, but she couldn't let this get away from her.

Greta locked her gaze on her. "I need to know,

is it what it looks like?"

Of course it was. Hell, it was so much more. But could she throw away her entire career for that? On the other hand, could she deny how she actually felt? What if Scott didn't feel the same way? She just knew she couldn't deny it. Even thinking about doing that made her ill.

Greta sighed. "You're being audited. All of your accounts, all of your interactions. You won't be given any new jobs until a determination is made. I know this isn't like you, so I don't know what happened. I'm hoping your record will speak for itself and give me some leeway, but it may not be my decision in the end. You're a well-known face for this company, and he's a well-known face in his industry, and with those photos out there, the general public knows one of our people crossed a very distinct line."

Kenzie stared at her clenched hands resting in her lap, knuckles white. She felt like a child being scolded. Her voice was quiet. "I understand."

chapter eighteen

Kenzie lay on her side, staring at her clock and watching the minutes tick away. Seven a.m.

7:01.

7:02.

She should get out of bed. Dress, get ready for the day. But for what? She didn't even know. She didn't have any meetings. May never have another meeting again.

She rolled her eyes at a knock on her bedroom door. "Go away."

Riley poked her head in the room. "I haven't seen you for days. Are you avoiding me? Oh geez, Kenz, what's wrong?"

The mattress shifted with the weight of a new body.

Kenzie sighed and rolled over, looking up at her sister sitting next to her, back against the headboard, studying her with concern.

"Nothing's wrong." Kenzie's lie came out as a dry croak.

Riley raised her eyebrows in disbelief. "Liar."

Kenzie pulled her comforter over her head. It was stifling under the covers, but she didn't want to face anyone. "Go away."

Riley yanked the blankets back. "No."

Kenzie glared at her, eyes narrow, trying to pour as much irritation into the expression as she could.

Riley stared back, not blinking.

Kenzie shook her head and rolled onto her side again, back to her sister. "I'm not talking about it."

Silence. Kenzie almost looked, but she resisted the urge to see what her twin was up to.

"Then I'll guess." Riley said. "It couldn't be because of the work thing because who would be upset about not having to work and still getting paid for it?"

Kenzie flopped back over, glaring at her sister. "I don't get paid when I don't work, and yes, the *work thing* sucks."

The corner of Riley's mouth pulled up. "So you can say more than just *go away*."

Kenzie rolled her eyes. "Fine. I'll tell you what's wrong. The day you moved in, I approached some guy in a coffee shop that I'd seen almost every weekend but never dared talk to before. And then I continued the cycle of doing things I never do." Her throat constricted as she spit out the words, the memories stinging her eyes.

"And my life has been out of control ever since." Her voice cracked, and she bit back a sob. She hated him for that. Or herself. Or someone. For the way he'd made her feel, for the mistakes she'd made because of it, for not being able to forget it regardless of how badly it had screwed everything up.

Riley reached down and brushed a strand of hair

off Kenzie's forehead. Her voice was soft, sympathetic. "Has it really been that bad? I had no idea, I'm sorry."

"Yes, no, I don't know." Kenzie forced herself to sit up, focusing on not crying.

"So you two aren't a thing after all?" Riley plucked at a loose thread on the comforter. "Because he's really hot."

"No." Kenzie hated the taste of the word. "We're not."

"Why not?"

Sometimes she hated how childlike her sister was. Irritation flooded her. "Because it's not appropriate. Why do you even have to ask?"

"Don't snap at me." Riley's playful expression vanished, replaced by pursed lips. "I'm tired of you acting like you've got a stick up your ass just because I have a different perspective on the world than you. You stash your entire salary in savings—an amazingly admirable thing to do—so you can retire young, but still insist on keeping it a secret, subsisting off Ramen and your expense account so everyone thinks you're well-off." She splayed out her fingers as she ticked off list points.

"And now you're keeping your distance from a guy you didn't take your eyes off the entire evening—who never took his eyes off you—at that party thing of his, because why? Because it's not appropriate? Because he's not as polished as you like your guys? He sure cleaned up well. Maybe you're afraid you can't get him to sustain that."

Kenzie felt more ill as every thought she'd had about Scott spilled from her sister's lips.

Riley looked at her, mouth twisted in disbelief. "Do you do anything because you want to and not because someone else told you it was appropriate?"

Kenzie pulled her blanket over her head, not wanting to see the accusation reflected at her. It was worse than looking in a mirror. "You don't get it."

"Then explain it to me," Riley said.

"Just forget it." It wasn't worth the effort. "Get out."

"Fine." The mattress shifted again as Riley got up. "One more thing first?"

The change in her sister's tone penetrated Kenzie's haze of self-pity. She sat, curious gaze locked on Riley. "I'm listening."

Riley stared back from the doorway, hesitation shining in her eyes. She took a deep breath. "No one knows this, so please don't tell."

Kenzie's curiosity grew. "I promise."

Riley fiddled with her fingers, running her thumb over each nail in order and then repeating the nervous gesture. "I left Archer, not the other way around."

Kenzie's eyes grew wide. She wasn't sure why she was hearing the confession now, but even more she wondered, "Why didn't you tell me? What happened?"

Riley gave a short laugh. "He proposed."

"Wait, what?"

Riley shuffled her weight from one foot to the other, watching the carpet. "He proposed, I freaked out and left. I didn't tell anyone because you all already think I'm this flake who can't even keep a boyfriend, and this only proves it."

Kenzie opened her mouth to offer some kind of denial and reassurance.

"I didn't know why I told him no at the time." Riley cut her off. "He's nice enough, he's kind—all the adjectives a guy should have. But..." She blew a strand of blonde off her forehead.

"Then I saw you and Scott at that investor dinner. The way his eyes never quite left you, the respect in his voice when he talked to you, the fact that you're exactly the same way with him. Archer and I never had that. We might have some day, but seriously, I don't think any of my friends—married, attached, whatever—look at each other with the kind of adoration he directed at you. And you'd sacrifice that because of some self-declared, impossibly immovable definition of what is and isn't appropriate?"

A sharp pang dug into Kenzie's chest and tears pricked her eyelids. "I don't have a choice."

Riley shrugged and turned away. "I don't see a gun to your head." She left, closing the door behind her, the latch clicking shut and echoing like a shot in Kenzie's head.

Another layer of guilt sank over Kenzie. She'd known Riley wouldn't understand. She never did. It had to be this way. There weren't any other options. Her stomach clenched with despair, and her eyes burned.

As much as she wanted to, she couldn't just lay around forever. She pushed herself out of bed, shuffled the few short feet to her desk, and dropped into the mesh chair. Riley's words taunted her as she started her laptop.

Why was she even dwelling? That was what had gotten her in trouble in the first place—believing that life would be better if she learned how to let loose. A tiny part of her reminded her she probably wouldn't have gotten to know Scott the way she had if it hadn't been for that impulse.

She mentally scolded herself. Then she wouldn't have fallen for him, wouldn't have lost him, and wouldn't be aching now.

She opened a web browser in autopilot. A blank search-engine screen stared back at her. What was she doing? She started typing in the search box, and the predictive results scrolled link after link to car dealerships.

She clicked down to Scott Evans, Jr. She lost track of time as she jumped from one site to the next. A newspaper article about him entering rehab at sixteen for alcoholism. Junior high yearbook photos from a very private, very expensive finishing school. High school photos of a quarterback who led his school's team to their worst record in decades, obliterating the way the school had worshiped his father's football career.

And blurb after blurb from gossip and society sections of local papers, older ones mentioning the well-behaved pre-teen sliding into quiet, sullen, and then the son who had disowned his own father.

She didn't know where to focus her thoughts first. He knew it all—everything she'd been trying to teach him about how to dress, behave, socialize, draw positive media attention, he already knew it. She traced her fingers over a black-and-white photograph of Scott in high school. He looked so very miserable.

Then again, how happy could a person be having a lifestyle they didn't enjoy shoved down their throat on a daily basis? She dropped her head into her arms. No wonder he'd been so resistant. He'd even tried to tell her, and she hadn't listened.

It was true, her job had been to make him look good in front of the cameras, but had she gone too far trying to change how he appeared instead of doing the right thing and making them appreciate what he already was?

Damn it.

Scott grabbed his phone the moment it rang, hope and nausea churning inside. "Grant, how are you?"

"Better than you, my boy." The usual underlying chuckle was gone from Grant's voice. "You really screwed things up. Not just for you, but for that young lady."

The statement gnawed on another layer of his mood. He wanted to believe she had used him as much as he had enjoyed her, but she'd made it clear that most of their relationship was in his head.

Scott pushed the thoughts back before they could become the jumbled mess they had every time they'd surfaced over the last twenty-four hours. "I know. I need information."

Grant would know what he was talking about. "I can't give you specifics, I can only tell you the board is split down the middle. You've made a lot of influential men—people who expect everyone to take them seriously—believe you think their word is meaningless."

Shitshitshitshitshitshitshit. He bit back the curse. If they voted to fire him, he'd lose the second most important thing in his life.

Wait. First. Right?

Right. Because Kenzie wasn't in his life anymore. He sandbagged the flood of thoughts again. Not that he cared. Only intensely and painfully.

"I warned you about selling your soul." Grant's warm sympathy interrupted the rambling thoughts.

Scott snapped back to the conversation. "I know. But what was I going to do?"

"Buy it back."

That was the fail-safe. The loophole. Scott knew that, but he was still concerned. "Buying out and firing Cartee isn't going to convince the rest of the board I'm worthy of keeping my job."

Grant sighed. "You'd have to convince them Hank was the only real risk."

Scott's eyes grew wide at the thought. He'd found the proof he needed that Cartee had planted the photos, but they were still real pictures. Hank had done so much more than Scott ever expected. Scott had yelled and argued with his father for hours after he'd uncovered Hank's financial background, and he'd finally discovered the truth. Was it enough?

"What if I could show that Hank's money wasn't his? That he lied about his funding and intended to displace me from his first day on the board? Do I even have a chance of convincing them I'm sorry and turning their attention back on him?"

Through a series of shell companies and offshore accounts, his father had funded Hank's failing empire to force Scott out of his own company. Being disowned by his son had left a bitter taste in his mouth. He'd known he couldn't buy in as himself, but he hadn't had to. Hank had been quick to act as a face for Scott's father since he'd never liked Scott or his business practices.

"Men like me let our money and egos drive us. You've already proven you're worth the investment. If your apology is sincere and your proof is solid, you might have a chance."

Scott exhaled, a whisper of relief tickling his senses. "Thanks. I owe you."

"You haven't let me down yet." Grant's smile was almost visible over the phone.

Scott's mind was racing as he hung up. That was what he had to do; it all made perfect sense. Rae could make the numbers work to buy out Hank, and he would beg the board's forgiveness if that's what it took to win them back, especially if he could share the blame with Cartee. As long as it didn't mean denying what had happened with Kenzie. Please don't let them ask that of him. It was the one concession he wasn't willing to make.

He slouched back against the couch, exhaustion rushing in to temper the exhilaration. So that was half his problem solved. What was he going to do about the other half?

He couldn't ask Kenzie for forgiveness. Listening to her tear him down again was too painful a road for him to even consider. But he knew how to save his own job, at least he could try to do the same for her. He placed another call.

Two hours later he was sitting in a small office across from a woman who insisted he call her Greta. Papers were piled high on either side of her, and loose strands of red rebelled against her ponytail.

Reporting to her must drive Kenzie insane. The thought would have made him smile on any other day.

"You're a lot more trouble than someone in your position should be." There was no malice in Greta's comment.

He let out a small laugh. "So I hear. Thank you for making time for me."

"Of course. You understand Mackenzie is one of my best, and I don't like the way this has turned out."

His gut clenched at the words, adding to the already churning dread of what he was about to say. He was going to sign away the last traces of something amazing, but he couldn't think of another way. "I don't blame you. I'm not so fond of it myself."

Her smile faltered. "I don't do small talk very well. Can we cut to the chase?"

"Right." He swallowed, mentally steeling himself. These ties needed to be severed completely, and this was the last missing piece. "Those pictures that got out. None of those were Miss Carter's fault."

He forced himself to keep talking. It destroyed him to admit it, but he knew it was true. "She was never anything but professional. She went above and beyond when it came to putting up with my crap. I was difficult, and I sabotaged her efforts for selfish reasons that had nothing to do with her or your organization."

Which was exactly the case, right? He had to convince himself he believed it, or it would show. He was a terrible liar.

Greta studied him for a moment. "You know this has legal implications, right? You leave yourself open to a harassment lawsuit if Mackenzie says it's appropriate. Breach of contract. Libel concerns."

He did. "I'm willing to go through whatever arbitration is necessary."

Her eyes narrowed. "It may be more serious than that."

His smile turned hard. "Then your contract should have covered that. What did it say? All claims and disputes arising under or relating to this agreement are to be settled by binding arbitration."

Not that he planned on dragging such a thing out, but he was willing to stick his ass on the line for Kenzie, not for a loosely worded, boiler-plate clause.

Greta's expression didn't give anything away. "Point taken. Thank you for stopping by."

He paused halfway out of his seat, not wanting to ask but not able to help himself. "This gets her out of hot water, right?"

Greta's mask slipped, a whisper of a genuine smile leaking in. "I can't guarantee anything, and I can't discuss that with you."

Of course. He knew better. "Thank you for your time."

chapter nineteen

Would it ever get easier to approach those giant glass walls that exposed the office to the rest of the world with no shame? Kenzie pushed the question aside. It didn't matter. After today she'd never do it again.

The receptionist glanced up as she approached, smile not as friendly as it had been in the past, but still polite. "Mr. Johnston says you can go on back."

Mr. Johnston. That didn't bode well. Kenzie returned the smile, hoping her nervousness didn't show. She couldn't tell Scott what she'd figured out, not that he would take her calls anyway, but she couldn't face him. Still, she had to tell someone and Zach seemed like as good an option as anything, so she'd set up a meeting with him.

She reached the office. It was the same basic layout as Scott's, but instead of industry awards, artwork, and framed magazine articles on the walls, it was sterile like the lobby. Her feet froze to the floor when she saw one of the two chairs across from Zach's desk was already occupied.

Zach stood and gestured to the empty chair. "Miss Carter. I hope you don't mind, we're in the middle of some serious planning, but I've got time for you. Have a seat."

Scott never looked at her. She struggled not to stare at his back, the T-shirt with a faded Sonic the Hedgehog, the torn jeans, everything that indicated he was him and not playing the role he'd been forced into. "Thank you, but I'll stand if that's all right. I won't take long."

Zach clasped his hands behind his back, rocking on his toes. "Suit yourself. What can I do for you?"

She opened her mouth, and her entire rehearsed speech evaporated from her thoughts. She hadn't meant to do this in front of Scott. He wasn't meant to hear this. What if he hated her for it?

Zach watched her expectantly.

She was going to have to say something. "I think you made a mistake hiring me." The words tumbled out before she knew what she was going to say. She wanted to flinch, but she was afraid if she stopped talking, she'd never be able to start again. "Not me specifically, but in general."

Zach raised an eyebrow but didn't interrupt.

"You have a brilliant designer, developer, director, person driving the creative half of this company." She forced herself not to look at Scott the entire time. "Regardless of what some suit on the board of directors says, he makes you what you are. And you can't make him conform just because people say he should. You can't stifle him."

She took a deep breath, hating the silence in the room. Should she say more? What else was she going to say? Short of proclaiming how very desperately she personally wished she could take it all back, if only she had recognized how she felt about him sooner … but that wasn't for public consumption. Or at least, not unless they both felt the same way.

Zach looked away from her, gaze falling to Scott, something unreadable in his expression.

She followed his line of sight, staring at the back of the impassive head.

Scott stood and turned, face a blank mask. His voice was cold, lined with a sharp edge. "It's my understanding, Miss Carter, that your company has assigned someone else to work with me."

At his request. Kenzie swallowed, the lack of emotion devouring her as much as the formality. "That's correct."

Scott's smile looked like it had been chiseled from ice. "Your employer might not appreciate you undermining their work. Especially since, if I'm correct, you still got paid."

The words sliced through her. She'd expected a lot of reactions, but not to be told she was wrong. To have her concession thrown back in her face. She opened her mouth to protest.

Scott cut her off. "You were right to begin with, Miss Carter. This is for the best. You can see yourself out, I assume?"

Hurt coursed through her, making every inch of her ache. "Yes. I'm sorry to have wasted your time."

His expression cracked, but she didn't stay to see if it crumbled. She spun on her toe, making a straight line for the exit and hoping she could hold back the tears until she was alone in her car.

♥ ♥ ♥

After Kenzie left, Scott dropped back into the chair, her words bouncing around in his skull, echoing with sincerity. Fuck, why did she have to do that? He was trying to forget how very much he wanted her, and she had to go and say those awful, kind words that made him want her even more, and still weren't enough to convince him she felt the same.

It had devoured him to be so cold, but she was only interested in making professional amends—he couldn't let himself believe otherwise, it already hurt too much. It was better this way. She was gone now, and he could begin what was already an agonizing process of getting over her. If he could.

Zach sat down too, a heavy sigh echoing through the room. "God, you're an ass sometimes."

Scott glared at him. "I didn't ask you."

Zach shrugged. "Which is funny, because I didn't ask to play middleman in some twisted kind of lovers' spat. We don't always get what we want."

"That's clever. Did you steal that off a Hallmark card?" Scott couldn't keep the snide from his question. "Seriously? What was the point of even hiring her? Cartee completely turned it against me. That's going to cost me a fortune."

"Your girl did her job and she did it well, aside from a couple indiscretions. Don't blame this on her." Zach drummed his fingers on the desk, rolling a loose cigarette back and forth across his knuckles.

"My girl?" The term crawled under Scott's skin, filling him with a despair he didn't understand.

Zach's expression didn't shift. "You're sure you want to take care of Cartee alone? Rae showed me the numbers. It's going to kill you to buy him out."

The clause they'd written into every investor's agreement. The one that allowed them to buy the person out for a fixed percentage above their original investment in exchange for removing them from the board of directors. The insurance they'd built in to make sure they didn't lose their company again. "I'm sure. This really is my fault. I won't let you pay for that."

Zach pursed his lips. "You really are a childish, spoiled brat. Even when you're taking responsibility, you have to play the martyr to prove a point."

Scott shrugged, wishing the words didn't hurt so much. "Frequently. And?"

"You got what you wanted, and in the end you get to do it your way, regardless of the cost. She's gone, you keep your job, and that painful irritation who calls himself Hank Cartee will be out of our lives.

"And you still look like someone shot your dog. You're not going to let a silly little girl saying things you've already proven distract you from that victory are you?"

He couldn't ignore it anymore. Scott knew what he wanted and for the first time in a long time, he suspected she was the one thing he couldn't have. "Yeah, I probably am."

"You love her."

Love. Was that what this was? If so, it hurt like hell. And he never wanted to lose it. "Pretty sure, yeah."

Zach's mask slipped, a whisper of a smile

leaking in. "You going after her?"

Not likely. "She doesn't want me."

"You're a moron. Of course she wants you."

She didn't. She couldn't. Not after everything that had happened between them. She hadn't even called him personally to share her "revelation." She'd gone to his business partner. Kept it public so—he could only assume—she wouldn't have to face how he might feel personally.

Kenzie sat in her car staring at the roof, not able to bring herself to leave the parking garage. Tears stung her eyelids, and her throat was raw. She was never going to see him again. Not after the way he'd dismissed her moments earlier.

And it was her fault. So many things she never should have done. Taken the contract. Denied how attracted she was to him. Convinced herself she'd be happy hiding something as amazing from the world as what she felt for him.

Not that any of that mattered now. Not that she'd recognized it before it was too late. Still, she could do one more thing. She could at least take responsibility for her part in what had happened. If nothing else, she could stop pretending he was the only guilty party.

She wouldn't even deserve the memories if she couldn't admit that. Before the thoughts finished forming, she was dialing.

"Hey." Greta's abrupt voice greeted her. "What's up?"

"This thing, this suspension." Kenzie dove right

in. It was the best way to get it out, and Greta would appreciate the direct approach. "It's my fault."

"Really?"

Kenzie didn't know how to interpret the question, so she just kept talking. "I mean, obviously, it takes two people, right? But I had been involved with the client before they signed me, and I should have said no then, or handed responsibility over to someone else at so many other points along the way. I'm sorry."

"Hmm."

That wasn't good. Kenzie waited, toe tapping faster with each second of silence that stretched between them.

"You're sure," Greta finally said.

What was Kenzie missing? "Positive."

"Here's the thing." Greta's voice softened. "Your *it takes two* was in here a couple of days ago, telling me personally that this was all *his* fault. That he sabotaged everything and set you up to fail."

Her heart stopped, and then kick started again, hammering against her ribs as she tried to make sense of it. "He said that?"

Greta laughed. "He also quoted contract at me when he told me he wouldn't allow any disputes to go beyond arbitration. And asked if you could have your job back. He's a force to be reckoned with, isn't he?"

She felt a smile forming for the first time in days, but it was subdued by the reality that it didn't matter what he'd done or why, she'd still never see him again. "He is."

"So here's the deal," Greta said. "I can consider

this conversation off the record. We can say it never happened if you'd like to agree to his version of events."

That would be convenient. Solve a lot of issues. Except the big outstanding one. Kenzie shook her head at the empty car. "I can't do that. I'm as much to blame as anyone. All I can say is it won't happen again." Because just then she couldn't imagine ever getting over Scott.

"I understand." Greta sounded sad. "I don't know if I can do anything for you if that's the case, but your record still speaks in your favor. I'll let you know as soon as I hear anything."

"Thanks." Kenzie disconnected and tossed her phone back in her purse. She still ached deep inside, and she hated the empty pit, but at least she'd finally stopped hiding things from everyone, including herself.

chapter twenty

Kenzie turned the folded clothes over in her hands, focused on the fabric of the T-shirt against her palms, the rough fleece of the battered sweats, the scent of detergent that wasn't hers and sent waves of need and regret through her.

She should probably give Scott his clothes back. She'd been in such a hurry to get out of them, so furious and hurt the morning he'd loaned them to her, that she'd set them aside in a little stack on the back corner of her desk, pretending they didn't exist.

She should wash them first. That would be the polite thing to do. But if she was washing them anyway, he wouldn't care if … no, she shouldn't. Screw it. It was as close as she was going to get to him ever again. She pulled the shirt over her head, inhaling deeply.

She tugged the sweats on next, having to pull the drawstring tight and roll the waistband down to let it rest comfortably on her hips.

She flopped back on her bed, staring at the ceiling, hugging herself. Her phone was in her hands before she knew why. Her fingers hesitated, the phone shaking along with her nerves. She had to do it. She missed him too much. She forced herself to type out the message.

I'm sorry.

No response. Of course, she didn't know what he was up to. He may not be somewhere he could answer. Or, more likely, he just wasn't going to. When her phone buzzed, she almost jumped straight up. She fumbled for the device, heart hammering, and pulled up the message.

Yeah. Me too.

Then nothing else. She should have expected that. It still hurt though. She really had destroyed her chances, hadn't she? Finally, a guy she got along with, who listened, who showed her the world from a perspective she'd never see it from on her own, and who had the most brilliant way with sexy words. Damn it.

She pulled her knees to her chest and rolled onto her side. Tears pricked her eyelids. This was it; she had ruined it. She had met the perfect guy, and instead of recognizing it, she'd drilled it into him over and over again that she was embarrassed by his very existence. No wonder he hated her.

She didn't know how long she stared blankly at the wall, listening to cars outside, the horns, the sounds of afternoon traffic, kids running through the halls, things that didn't matter anymore.

A knock echoed through the room, startling her from her reverie. She wiped an arm across her eyes, not doing anything but making them rawer, and shuffled out of her bedroom toward the front door. She swung it open without bothering to check the peep hole. Why should she bother?

Her eyes grew wide when she saw Scott. He stood in front of her in the most expensive suit she'd ever seen, tailored to fit his broad shoulders and narrow waist, ivory cuff links peeking out past the end of the jacket sleeves.

"Oh, my gawd. You look amazing." The compliment slipped out before she could stop it.

His crooked smile spread across his face, and he grasped her fingers between his. He kissed the back of her hand. "Thank you, Miss Carter. You look stunning too. You wear that far better than I ever did."

Heat crept across her cheeks, and she ducked her head. She looked horrible. Face blotchy without makeup, hair in a ponytail. He didn't mean it.

He wrapped an arm around her waist, resting his hand at the small of her back, and pulled her closer. He kissed her softly, lips undemanding, but hungry. He broke away, resting his forehead against hers. "You really, really do look incredible. The best thing I've ever seen. Do you have a minute?"

She hesitated. What was he up to?

Before she could think of a response, he'd grabbed her purse and keys off the table by the door and kicked her sandals in her direction. He slipped his hand around hers and tugged. "I have a surprise for you."

A shock of want raced through her, and she bit it back. She wasn't able to suppress the hope so easily. She allowed herself to be led down to the street toward a silver Porsche convertible. "This isn't your car."

He held the door open, waiting patiently. "I

borrowed it from a friend. It's a little classier than the love van. He was always better at that than me."

The faint scent of cigarette smoke mingled with flowers from a hidden air freshener. Zach's car. Too many questions assaulted her, and she didn't know which to ask first.

He pulled into traffic, demeanor still friendly but aloof. His fingers brushed her leg through her sweats, lingering for a moment before he pulled away again.

He glanced at her, a hint of worry finally leaking into his deep eyes. "Say something?"

She should do that. But she didn't even know where to start. "Why didn't you tell me about your past?" That wasn't where she wanted to start. She wanted to apologize. To tell him they could make it work. Instead, the accusation was out there with no way to take it back.

He cringed. "It's not the kind of thing I like to dwell on. Even though I came from money, I wasn't coddled as a child, and I earned everything I have now. So to me, it's inconsequential."

She couldn't help the soft smile that slipped out. "That makes an amazing amount of sense. But you already knew everything I tried to tell you. Why did you let me put you through that?"

He took a deep breath and pulled the car into a nearby parking spot. His voice was soft, and he never looked at her. "You'll hate me if I tell you."

The quake in his voice filled her with concern and regret. She kept her tone reassuring. "I really doubt that."

He continued, gaze locked straight ahead. "I

hired you specifically because I needed to look like I was complying with my board, and I really didn't want to. I thought I could distract you, screw around a little, and not actually have to follow anyone's rules but my own."

She didn't know what to say. Didn't even know if she could speak. There had been times she'd expected as much, but it still hurt to hear it.

He glanced at her, but didn't turn his head. "And then I was so very wrong. You're amazing at what you do, despite how stubborn I am, and I still can't believe you put up with me from day one. And you were right. I do need to watch myself sometimes. You've reminded me that even though I do this for the freedom of building my dream and sharing it, sometimes I have to compromise.

"But even if I play nice, I don't play fake to impress people." He finally turned in his seat, facing her, brown eyes raking over her face. "Did you mean what you said in Zach's office?"

"Yes." The answer thrummed in her chest. Every word of it. "No one should force you into a mold. It would break you. It would destroy something amazing." Her voice caught on the last few words.

He rested a finger under her chin, drawing her face closer. His mouth hovered less than an inch from hers, his voice barely audible. "That would be a shame, wouldn't it?"

Her breath hitched. He dropped his hand and backed away. Disappointment flooded her.

He was out of the car and standing next to her, door open and hand out, before she could decide if she was irritated or just hurt.

She accepted the offer of help, focusing on how his palm rested firmly against hers. She stepped next to him on the sidewalk and realized they were in front of his building.

"Come on." He tugged her toward the lobby, nodding at the doorman as he guided her toward the elevator.

"Where are we going?" The ups and downs, the pendulum of emotions, the jittery nature of the conversation, they all made her head spin. She'd missed that about being around him.

He intertwined his fingers with hers, not looking at her. "Presumably, my condo."

The car slid to a stop, and the doors opened. Her stomach couldn't take much more of this. "That's not an answer."

He stepped into the hallway, trying to tug her after him. "You'll see."

She planted her feet. "Tell me now."

He pulled. "At least let the elevator go so someone else can use it."

She twisted her mouth in irritation, but stepped into the hallway, doors sliding shut behind her. "I'm waiting."

His mask crumbled, and worry, uncertainty, and something else she couldn't read flooded his face. He pulled her closer, fingers still intertwined with hers, his other hand resting on her neck, thumb against her cheek. His quiet voice echoed in the empty hallway. "I'm not keeping quiet to frustrate you, I promise. I want you to know everything about me because I want to know everything about you. I want you in my life. No, that's not right. I need you. Desperately and completely. I crave your company and your touch." He dropped his hand, grazing the violet that hung around her neck. "And all of you."

Her chest throbbed, and she thought it might burst. She could only manage two words in response. "Me too."

He brushed his lips over hers and pulled away, apprehension and hope on his face. "Yeah?"

She laughed and nodded. It still felt amazing around him. Even more so now. "Yeah."

He dipped in for another kiss, and she rested a finger on his lips. "But," she said. Hurt radiated in his eyes. Gawd those eyes. She could get lost in them. "You still haven't told me what you're up to."

"Oh." He grinned and tugged her ponytail, yanking her head back. He raked his teeth up her throat, stopping at her ear with a nibble. His breath was warm against her skin when he whispered, "Dinner."

She wanted to sink into the gesture. She could spend forever wrapped in his arms. But she also couldn't let him get away with such a vague answer. "Dinner in an empty hallway?"

"Dinner at my place." He tugged her toward the door.

She followed without protesting, curiosity piqued. Besides, she was enjoying his hand on hers and watching the enthusiasm that drove him, so she didn't want to pull away.

She gasped at the sight that met her when they pushed inside. Against the back balcony sat a table for two, complete with unlit candles, with the twinkling city lights in the twilight of the entire city as the background. "It's beautiful."

He kicked the door shut, and it latched behind them. "You definitely are."

She turned and realized he was watching her, not the scenery. She ducked her head, hoping to hide the heat rushing through her face.

He tilted her head up again, finger under her chin, and pressed his mouth to hers. The kiss was firm, hungry.

She gasped and her lips parted. His tongue darted between her teeth, intertwining with hers. His hand rested at the small of her back, holding her close. He broke away, but didn't let her go, eyes dark and holding her captive.

She pressed closer. "So you rich boys really do get room service?"

He tightened his grip on her waist. "I thought I'd cook for you."

She raised an eyebrow. "You cook?"

"You learn to make do when the only thing you can afford is flour, water, and ramen. Nothing impressive. Just pizza."

"Candlelit dinner with homemade pizza. Only you." She loved the idea. But the air smelled distinctly unlike baking food. "You haven't cooked it yet."

He grazed his teeth over her shoulder. "It's in the fridge. I didn't know if you'd actually come with me."

He was just as uncertain about the entire thing as she was. She intertwined her fingers behind his head and rested her hands against the back of his neck. Her pulse screamed, need pouring through her and reflecting his expression. "So, dinner can wait?"

His voice was deep, desperate. "What did you have in mind?"

She trailed a finger up his chest and brushed it across his lips before following with her own. "Guess."

He dipped quickly, his other arm wrapping around her knees and lifting her off her feet. She gasped as her world shifted and tightened her grip around his neck, resting her head on his chest.

With just a few steps, he crossed the room, pushed into his bedroom, and set her gently on the bed.

She lay back, propped up on her elbows. "What would you have done if I said no?"

He hovered over her, one hand on either side of her head, legs straddling hers. "I hadn't thought that far. It hurt too much." He dipped his head, lips grazing her neck. "But you still have a chance to back out." His words vibrated against her skin.

She arched her back, sighing at his touch. "I'm good here, thanks."

chapter twenty-one

He rolled to one side, mouth still exploring her neck and throat, and his free hand dropped to her waist. He pushed her shirt aside enough to rest his fingers on her bare hip. "I'm not sure I remember how to do this."

She snickered. "You're going to have to be more specific."

His hand glided up her side, thumb on her stomach and then brushing the bottom of her breast.

She whimpered and arched her back.

"You know." His breath was warm against her skin. "Private place, both of us in the same bed, no timers or threat of interruption."

She pulled his face to hers and kissed him deeply, gasping when they broke apart. "I'm sure you'll figure it out. You're creative and resourceful."

He trailed his mouth down her throat again and then pushed her shirt up, lips soft against her stomach. He followed a trail back up her bare chest, feather light kisses drawing a random pattern.

She let out a tiny sigh, the almost ticklish sensation making her lightheaded.

He kissed the bottom of one breast and then the

other, moving back and forth until he reached a nipple. She inhaled sharply when his tongue flicked over one nub before taking it into his mouth.

He sucked and nibbled, and she squirmed closer, currents of enjoyment rippling through her like that single spot was attached to a string connected to every other erogenous zone on her body.

He sought out the other one with his hand, kneading the fleshy mound, the pad of his thumb brushing the swollen flesh.

She gasped under the attention but wanted more. Nudging his shoulder, she pushed him onto his back and then rolled so she was straddling him. His eyes raked over her appreciatively, smile widening when she pulled her shirt off and tossed it aside.

His hands glided up her sides, cupping her breasts again, pinching and pulling her nipples.

She whimpered and ground against him, his excitement pressing back through slacks and sweats. Sliding down his body, she undid each button on her way, pushing his shirt aside as her mouth explored his chest, his stomach, until she reached his waist.

He groaned when her fingers slid under his waistband. She raked her palms over his skin as she yanked off his pants and boxers, exploring every inch of his upper thighs except the eight or so begging for her attention.

His breathing grew more jagged, catching every time she drew closer. She stepped off the bed long enough to drop the rest of her clothes to the floor.

He propped himself up, eyes raking over her in appreciation. "You're so beautiful."

The compliment warmed her as much as his gaze did, heat flooding every inch of her.

He sat on the edge of the bed, tugging her to rest between his legs, but leaving her standing. He threw his shirt aside, and then his hands found her ass. He pulled her closer, lips pressing into her stomach, her hips, back up to her breasts. His fingers moved lower, parting her lips, drawing a moan as they glided along her already slippery slit.

He caught a swollen nipple between his teeth, scraping the flesh and flicking with his tongue. She shuddered and pressed closer, trying to focus on every touch at once. His thumb rested against her clit, and she arched her back, grinding on his hand as he stroked.

From behind, his other hand found her eager opening, and she cried out when one finger slid inside, and then another. Her hips bucked against his expert attentions as he pumped, stroked, and sucked, and her gasps became short pants as pleasure washed through her. She cried out as she climaxed, riding the wave until he slowly pulled away.

She dipped her mouth to his, kissing him with hunger before pushing him onto his back again. He slid completely onto the bed, and she followed, hovering over him, straddling his legs.

His fingers tangled in her hair, and he pulled her close, breath hot on her ear. "Condoms, end table, top drawer."

She shook her head, kissing him, teeth scraping his bottom lip. "You're clean?"

His crooked smile looked wicked when it was tainted with lust. He nodded. "You? Birth control?"

"Yes and yes." She wanted to feel all of him against her, inside her, with nothing in the way. She rocked against him, letting his hard length glide against her slit, her gasps mingling with his moans.

He moved his mouth along her throat, tongue tracing lines over her collarbone. "This is incredible." A familiar growl cut through his pants. "But goddammit, please?"

She couldn't hide her smile at the desperation, and it heightened her arousal that it was as intense as her own need. She sat straight up, pausing with his head hovering at the edge of her hole.

He grunted and thrust up. She cried out when he pushed inside her, a wave of intensity screaming through every inch of her.

His hands rested on her upper thighs, thumbs stroking the soft skin. She rocked slowly against him, sighing every time he drove deep inside her.

One of his hands moved higher, thumb finding her clit again, and she almost recoiled at the touch on still-sensitive skin. He brushed lightly, and her pace increased. His hips slammed against her, and he stroked around the tender bud.

His shallow breathing matched her own. Her head grew light as climax rolled through her again, taking her right to the edge, but not letting go. He pounded hard inside her, and his thumb continued to work her over.

His grunts filled the room, mingling with her gasps. His pace quickened, and he slammed into her. She hovered near orgasm, pleasure stealing her oxygen, making her head swim.

His hand tightened on her thigh when he came,

but his pace didn't slow. Her body relented, and she peaked, climax screaming through her.

She slowed and then stopped as he did, dropping her cheek onto his chest, struggling to catch her breath, and letting his hammering heart and raspy gasps echo in her head.

His fingers raked through her hair, his other hand tracing soft patterns along her spine. She giggled at the ticklish sensation.

"You're so incredible." His words rumbled through her ear. "I don't know what I would have done if you'd told me to go to hell when I showed up at your door."

She smiled, sitting up enough to brush her lips over his, and then rolled off to lie next to him before resting her cheek on his chest again. "Honestly? The thought never even crossed my mind."

"Never?"

"Not even for a millisecond." She complied when he pulled her closer, pressing completely against him and wrapping her leg over his.

♥♥♥

Kenzie snuggled into the bare chest behind her, enjoying his skin against hers, and pulled his arm over her, kissing his knuckles. She hadn't slept that well in forever. She could get used to waking up like this. In his bed, wrapped in his arms and flannel sheets.

His low chuckle rumbled through her back. "That's nice."

"Mhm." She brushed her lips over the pads of his fingers. "You know what else would be nice?"

His teeth grazed her shoulder. "I can think of a few things."

She moaned and squirmed against him, his arousal pressing into her butt. "I was thinking something of an entirely different nature, but my idea can wait."

"Nope." He pulled her close, breath warm on her neck. "Tell me."

She was almost reluctant to lose the moment. Except she suspected she wouldn't. "I think it would be nice if you bought me breakfast."

"I already told you." His words vibrated against her skin. "I don't get room service. It's a condo, not a hotel."

She smiled at the hint of hesitation in his tease. "I know. But at some point you mentioned a diner. And I love French toast."

"Yeah?"

She rolled onto her back so she could look up at him. "Yup."

"You'd suffer the public humiliation of going out in my clothes, with scruffy me, for free breakfast?" A smile danced behind his eyes, destroying his otherwise serious expression.

"I'd suffer the possibility of bad French toast to let the world know what an amazing man I'm dating."

"Are we?" He studied her.

"Dating? Gawd I hope so." She lifted her head long enough to press her lips to his before flopping back again. "I'm entirely too smitten to settle for anything less."

"Plus I'm amazing in bed." He brushed the

outside of her ear with his fingers.

Her laugh faded to a happy sigh as she sank into the gesture. "Plus that."

He rested a hand on her stomach. "Okay, breakfast on one condition."

She tried to give him a look of disbelief, but she knew her smile was ruining it. "Which is?"

He sat and took her hands in his. "Move in with me."

Her laugh was cut short when she realized he was serious. She sat also, not sure how she felt about the idea. "I … but … you can't just ask something like that out of the blue."

He shrugged. "Why not? Let Riley take over your place or something. It'll make things easier until you get work straightened out."

For some reason his logic dug at her insecurities. This wasn't because he felt guilty about her job was it? "Is that the only reason you're offering?"

He faltered, pink creeping over his face, and he turned away. His "No" was so soft she wasn't sure she heard it.

His shoulders rose and fell, and he met her gaze again. "I want you here. I adore you, I need you, I don't want to send you home at night, and I love you."

Those last three words caught her off guard, and she slid into a defensive response. "You don't know me." The hurt on his face told her that hadn't been the best approach. She kept talking, hoping to make him understand. "I don't know you. It's only been a couple months."

He raised an eyebrow. "With the size of that file your agency has on me, you know more about me than my mother."

Why was she fighting this? Part of her was screaming at her to say yes, but she couldn't force the words out. "But not more about you than your friends. Not more than Zach or Rae."

"Bullshit." He scooted closer, resting his hands on her knees. "I mean, okay sure, there's probably little things you know that they don't and vice versa. Rae doesn't know about the mole on my ass."

Kenzie laughed, part of her hating that the rest of her relaxed at that comment. "But Zach does?"

"Maybe." He traced a finger over her bottom lip.

She wanted to close her eyes and lean into the gesture, but she wouldn't be distracted. "They know when you lost your virginity."

Scott raised an eyebrow. "They think they know. They don't."

Her curiosity was piqued. "Do tell."

"Zach will tell you it was when I was fifteen. Some party at my parents' house while they were out of town. He set me up, I was too nervous and told her no, and she had already bragged to her friends and didn't want to take it back. So I let people believe it too."

She had to know. "Tell me it wasn't Rae."

He shook his head, face twisted in a smirk. "No, we don't have that kind of relationship. It happened when I was twenty-one."

"Bullshit." She mimicked his earlier objection. "You were gorgeous and popular in high school.

There's no way women weren't throwing themselves at you."

He shrugged. "To be fair, I wasn't inexperienced by that point. *Losing my virginity* is a technicality. Besides, I was miserable as a teenager, uncomfortable with who I was pretending to be, and frequently drunk."

The story was captivating. She had to know more. "How did it happen?"

"It was my twenty-first birthday, and the first one in almost a decade where I wasn't completely wasted off my ass. I was in a bar, staring at a bottle of beer, wondering if turning twenty-one was a good excuse to break five months on the wagon."

She bit back her comments about being the only person she'd ever met who intentionally stayed sober on his twenty-first birthday.

He continued. "There was a woman there, and she wasn't having such a great time either. We started talking, she ditched her friends, and I ended up in her bed. I couldn't tell you her name, but I can tell you I wasn't her first by any stretch of the imagination."

She wasn't sure how to respond. She liked seeing this side of Scott. Open and vulnerable. But when she thought about it, he'd always been open with her.

"So you almost managed to change the subject." He scooted away, breaking any contact between them. "Is that your way of telling me no without actually having to say it?"

She shook her head and closed the distance between them, wrapping her arms around his neck.

"It's not. My answer is yes. I'd love to not have to go home at night. And I…" she hesitated on the words, and then realized the normal terror that went with them wasn't there. "I love you too."

♥♥♥

"Is this seat taken?" A familiar voice cut through the din of the coffee shop.

Scott looked up from his game—not that he'd been able to focus anyway—frowning when he couldn't read Kenzie's expression. He rose enough to brush his lips over hers, heartbeat increasing when she let the kiss linger. He still hadn't gotten used to that, and with any luck he never would.

He locked his gaze on hers as she took the chair next to him, still not able to read her. She'd stepped away to take a call from work. Before she left, he managed to gather they'd finally made a decision about how to handle the public embarrassment he'd stuck her—and them—with.

The corners of her mouth turned down, and she looked away. She ignored the tea he'd ordered for her, stealing his coffee instead and taking a long drink before handing it back. She wouldn't meet his gaze.

His stomach sank, mind already racing through lists of contacts who might be able to hook her up. Not that she needed him to call in any favors; she had an amazing résumé, but he had to do something to help. "How bad is it?"

Her somber expression cracked, and she giggled.

Uncertain relief nudged some of his dread

aside.

She kissed him deeply, hand resting on his knee for balance, tongue dancing around his. When she broke away, her entire face was smiling, pink tingeing her cheeks.

"You're a pest." He couldn't force any irritation into his voice. "Tell me."

She took another sip of his coffee. "This is good. Hazelnut? I would have pegged you as too manly for anything but straight, black, harsh-as-tar coffee."

"Yes. I've got a soft, gooey center that no one knows about except anyone who's ever talked to me for longer than a few minutes, which means I like my coffee sweet." He rested his palms on either side of her face, holding it in place. "You're killing me, you know that, right?"

She laughed. "I'm sorry. It went fantastically. I'm still on probation, but Greta is putting me back in the queue for new clients. They're being lenient, enforcing the spirit of the law instead of the letter, because one, I've never done it before, and two, now that I have someone amazing around to keep me in line, I'm not going to do it again."

He raised an eyebrow. "You never told me it was my job to keep you in line. I don't even do that for myself."

"I've noticed." She shook her head with amusement, tracing a finger over the bare skin peeking through his ripped jeans.

He growled at the light touch, teeth grazing her neck. "Maybe we should take off. Go somewhere less public."

She tilted her head to the side, bottom lip caught between her teeth as she studied him. "The back of the love van?"

The playful expression taunted and relieved him. "I was thinking home, but I guess that depends on if I can keep my hands to myself for that long."

She stood and tugged his arm. "Sounds like a challenge."

His pulse screamed. She didn't strike him as the kind of woman to back away from a challenge.

The End

If you'd like to see what happens to Riley, when her best friend Zane returns from deployment in the Air Force, check out *Her Airman*. Keep reading for a free sneak peek of chapter one

her airman

chapter one

Car exhaust and espresso. It smelled so wrong, but for Zane, it was almost perfect. Only one thing was missing. He scanned the cars passing the wooden shack, which was barely big enough for a coffeemaker and a couple of employees. *Where's Riley?*

It was April, too early in the year for many people to be occupying the plastic benches surrounding the drive-up coffee shop. He grabbed their drinks from the barista, knowing what kind of coffee she'd want, and picked one of the empty tables to set the cups down on.

He tapped his toes inside his shoes in time with the passing seconds. Why was he so on edge? Aside from the obvious *my past haunts my every waking and sleeping moment.*

Was he really nervous about seeing Riley

again? Okay, so he'd been deployed in the Air Force for the past six years, but they'd kept in touch. Email, hanging out when he was on leave, and chatting online whenever possible.

Oh, and those chats. Heat flooded his veins at the rush of pleasant memories. *Chatting* was a bit of an understatement. He'd barely been gone for a year when their conversations changed. Got more intimate.

Jesus. The things they'd said to each other, wrapped in excuses like *we're thousands of miles apart* and *it's just two friends helping each other out.* For the sake of their friendship he hoped those conversations wouldn't come between them now, but that didn't stop his fantasies from running rampant with images of stripping her down. Pinning her against the wall. Making her scream with pleasure…

He shook the vivid thoughts aside. The last thing he wanted was for this to cause a gaping rift between them when they were face to face.

His pocket vibrated and he reached for his phone. Was she canceling? He wasn't sure if that would be a relief or a disappointment. When he saw the messages, he rolled his eyes, his irritation surging. They weren't from Riley.

Checking in.

How's civilian life?

I'm in your part of the country. Meet me for coffee?

He glared at the phone. No matter how many times he told Sabrina he wasn't interested, she kept trying to recruit him.

And now the memories of his deployment were

back, along with emotions he'd rather not have. Guilt. Horror. Resignation. The thoughts tightened in his chest and danced in front of his eyes.

"Sexy love letters from your girlfriend?"

Riley's voice came from behind and jolted him back to the now. She wrapped her arms around his neck, her slender frame pressing into his back when she hugged him. She was almost as tall as he was, but experience told him she had to stand on tip-toe to do that. The familiar scent of cherry lip-gloss mingled with everything else and made it easier to stash his sins behind thoughts of her. Her breasts molded to him and rested against his shoulder blades.

He smiled and concentrated on falling into the sensations of her. "Hey, stranger."

"Hey, yourself." Riley settled her forehead against his shoulder. "Am I interrupting?"

It was easy to relax against her, as though with Riley's touch, the last six years faded. He pocketed his phone. He could tell Sabrina *no* for the fiftieth time later.

Zane spun to face Riley. "Not interrupting at all," he said. "I'm here for you." He couldn't stop from tracing his gaze over her. Fuck, was he here for her. Her long-sleeved T-shirt hugged round breasts, and her blonde hair framed a pixie-like face and a teasing smile. "How have you been?"

"Not nearly as great as I am right now." She locked her gaze on his, eyes bright blue and dancing with mischief. "I can't believe you're really back. For good. We have so much to catch up on. So much to do."

His sex-starved imagination seized and taunted

him with the concept of what they could be doing. When he pushed aside the mental images of tasting her cherry-flavored lips, they left an empty spot for a new tension to dive in. A pang clattered in his gut, bringing memories of what he'd left behind in the Air Force.

That was one bit of *catching up on* that could wait until later. Or never. She didn't need that kind of burden. He swallowed the response, not letting it show on his face. "What have you been up to?"

"This and that." She turned her attention to the ground, fingers flying to the silver heart resting at the base of her throat. She still had the locked he'd given her in high school. The *Friends Forever* one.

The realization warmed him. "That's specific."

"Is this for me?" She grabbed one of the cups from the table.

"Only if you still like caramel lattes."

"Only if you need air to breathe." She kissed him on the cheek, took a long drink, and then dropped onto the bench across from him, fiddling with the paper sleeve on the cup.

Apparently, he wasn't the only one with secrets. "The last few years have been so good you don't even want to talk about them?"

She met his gaze. "Wrong." Her voice was a combination of finality and teasing. "You're the one who dropped off the radar two years ago. You don't get to waltz back into town as if you were never gone, and interrogate me about my life without giving me details in return."

He really wanted to avoid this conversation. But he could redirect if needed. "What do you want to know?"

"Where are you staying?"

He could answer that question. "One of Archer's spare rooms. He's letting me have it cheap, until I find work."

Riley's expression shifted in an instant, as her furrowed brow melted into wide-eyed realization. "Really? And you're still wondering what I was up to?"

"Yes."

She gave a short laugh, but she didn't sound amused. "I'm kind of surprised he didn't mention it is all. We... Um... I was staying there for a while too."

That explained a lot. Riley and Archer, his two best friends, had a perpetual on-again, off-again relationship. "I thought you two were done." Funny how Archer didn't mention the on-again part of things when Zane mentioned where he was going this afternoon.

"We are, this time."

He'd heard that before. He raised an eyebrow.

"This is different from any other time," she protested. "Now. I answered your question. You answer mine. Give and take, right? Where did you go?"

Technically, nowhere. In truth, everywhere he hadn't wanted to. "Afghanistan. Iran. North Korea. You already know that." Her comment back then, when he gave her the basic details of his job, was *I always thought Air Force equaled being some hotshot, flying fighter jets. You really get to hone your hacking skills instead?* He'd told her it was called *intelligence*. Someone had to keep those hotshots safe in the air.

He should have stuck to doing exactly that. Guilt tried to worm its way back in, and he scrubbed it out. This gnawing shadow was going to be status quo for a while, wasn't it?

She clucked. "All of that happened before you dropped off the radar. Where have you been for the last two years?"

"How's the drawing coming?" He snatched the first topic he could think of. Riley was a brilliant artist. She kept saying she wanted to go pro. Step up and teach at the community college at least. Maybe try to publish one of her graphic novels.

While he was deployed, he'd happily sent her photos for reference shots—of him, of his Air Force buddies, all of it. Anything to help her with her passion.

"It's good. Now that you're back, you and your truck can model for me in person." She twirled her cup on the table. Her expression said she wasn't buying any of his attempts to change the subject. But she was letting him do it anyway.

"You drew my truck into your story?" It was an older model BMW 1602 he and Granddad converted into a truck when he was a teenager.

A hint of a smile crept back in. "It's got character. I love your truck. Your granddad let me take pictures whenever he pulled it out of storage for maintenance."

That made sense. Granddad adored Riley.

Silence fell between them. Their conversations had never been stilted, so why did the silence feel wrong, now? Because he was keeping secrets, and so was she. Why did she have to hook up with Archer? Again.

Not that Zane deserved a say in who Riley dated… And they never made him take sides, but it still made things awkward. "What else have you been up to?" he asked.

She clenched her jaw for the briefest of moments before her playful smirk returned. "There's not a lot to tell. Kenzie landed herself a sexy rich guy—you got a wedding announcement, right?—so I took over her condo payments. I'm thinking about buying it."

Which sounded fantastic, except for one teensy, tiny thing. "You hate living alone."

"I'm a big girl now. I can handle the scary noises. Speaking of…" She fiddled with her keys for a moment, before she finally pulled one from the ring. She leaned over the table and dropped the single key into his shirt pocket. "You're always welcome to stop by. It might be more comfortable hanging out at my place."

His cock stirred, and a desire seared over him when she glided her hands over his chest, and the way she bent at the waist gave him a fantastic view down the front of her shirt. Oh, so many shared fantasies.

She dropped back into her seat, toying with her hair, her gaze flitting everywhere. That felt out of place. It was like a dim image of what he remembered, but someone had missed something in the forgery. Her subtle discomfort didn't sit well with him. "Aren't you and Archer talking?"

Most couples that broke up tended to not speak, but Riley and Archer were different. They always made up when they weren't involved.

She turned her attention back to her drink. "We're working on it. It's still awkward, but friendship first. Right?"

"Always." Zane wouldn't overthink her question. Wouldn't wonder if she was talking about Archer, or about what she and Zane got up to.

This was why Riley never wanted to date Zane. She couldn't handle their friendship fracturing the way hers had with Archer. No one knew her better than Zane. She was so glad to have him back, she wasn't giving him up again.

Except this wasn't the Zane she hung out with years ago. The difference wasn't distinct, but he seemed more formal around her. Less at ease. And instinct told her it wasn't only because of the Archer mistake.

Please don't let it be the cybersex. The last thing she needed was to drive away her best friend because their online conversation got a little—or a lot—intense. Maybe once they got comfortable with each other again, it wouldn't be a big deal.

She and Zane had flirted since before they were old enough to realize they were doing it, and once upon a time, she thought he'd be her Prince Charming. She figured out years ago their relationship didn't work that way. He was the one man she felt comfortable saying that about. She could tease him all she wanted, and he gave as good as he got, but it didn't mean anything romantic.

"Does this whole *friendship first* thing mean I've lost my chance?" Zane stuck out his lower lip in an exaggerated pout, teasing dancing in his pale eyes.

As if. She laughed and shook her head. "Even if you didn't mean too much to me to just be some random hookup, I'm trying to change. I'm done falling for every guy who smiles at me."

"So, what? You're never dating again? Things might get a little lonely in the bedroom... You sure you can hold out?" Of course he had to go there.

Not that she minded the playful banter. This was so much better than sidestepping conversational landmines. "I've got a good vibrator. I've also got a lot better grasp on my desires than you and your so-called *celibacy*. We both know how not true that is."

His tiny smirk defied his attempt to look innocent. "I don't know what you're talking about. I haven't been with anyone since— Well, you know."

And... moment ruined. He meant Sabrina, the Air Force girlfriend. She still didn't know why he thought sleeping with a superior officer was a good idea. Riley studied him—the sturdy set of his jaw, the scruff of probably two days' worth of beard. *God,* he was sexy. "I didn't mean physically."

"Ah. Right." The corner of his mouth quirked up in a half-grin.

Riley was referring to all the times one of them had been lonely or horny, and their conversations became more than casual banter. "I'm guessing it's easier to hold out when you've got someone on call who you can talk dirty to."

"If you're saying that to cite my lack of

willpower, I wasn't always the one asking."

"Whatever. Now that you're back, the tail is going to be throwing itself at you. You won't need me anymore." It was supposed to be a teasing comment. Tossed out without meaning. But the words tasted sour in the back of Riley's throat.

"I will always and forever need you."

His reassurance burrowed deeper than she expected, reassuring and soothing nerves she hadn't realized was exposed. "Me too. I mean—"

"I know what you mean."

Of course he did. That was part of who they were. And now they could get back to normal. No worries.

The story continues in chapter two...